The Advanced RPG Beginners Guide to Becoming a Dungeon Master

An Easy-to-Digest Collection of Knowledge
for New Game Masters

Eric Heim & Alexander Cosic

Ebook ISBN: 978-1-965673-03-4

Paperback ISBN: 978-1-965673-04-1

Hardcover ISBN: 978-1-965673-05-8

Table of Contents

Introduction
Ignore the Man Behind the Screen

A thick mist envelops the players as they move through the old ruins of what was once a magnificent castle. There is little to see in the dark, so they must move about the ruins quietly and cautiously. The faint skittering of rats echoes from the walls as the players enter the once proud throne room. The door swings shut behind them, causing some to gasp and others to draw their weapons—fire dances from one wall sconce to the other, lighting the long corridor. Finally, the fire rests in the pit before the throne, highlighting the decaying corpse seated, slouched over in his spot. Creaking tendons click into place as his undead highness awakens. There is a soft voice from the heavens: "Roll for initiative."

In tabletop role-playing games (TTRPGs), the person running the game adds immersion, even if their voice sometimes falters. While everyone else plays, this person is in charge of the game.

In *Dungeons & Dragons*, this person is called the Dungeon Master (DM) but may have another name, such as Game Master (GM), depending on which game you play. They are an ideal mix of a god and a referee. Despite the grandeur behind what I just said, there is a bit of truth to it. But let's not get ahead of ourselves. Let's discuss some basics first.

Throughout this book, I will operate under the assumption that you understand the basic concepts of tabletop RPGs. If you are unfamiliar with these, you can purchase our previous book, *The Beginner's Guide to Role-Playing Games,* to quickly learn them before returning to this one. Therefore, I will not go into the details of gameplay mechanics and the other similar topics covered there, but I will still reference some basics here and there to give proper context. That book offers surface-level advice on running your own game, but I assume you are here to dive in and learn all about it.

Although this book is not aimed at total beginners, I will be operating under the assumption that you aspire to become a Dungeon Master and you are a total novice in that area. But be patient. Before getting into the meat of DMing, I'd like to give you a bit of an introduction to what you'll be learning.

In the beginning, I will explain some basic terminology. At this point, you may *already* be confused about the difference between a DM and a GM, but fear not; I plan to resolve that confusion straight away. Once we have that figured out, I will go into details about what a DM is and, more importantly, what a DM isn't, as I believe they are a vital distinction to be versed in before setting up your first game.

Then, I will give you a brief overview of how your station can be organized while you're running the game and will also give you a list of things you need to have planned and figured out before inviting your players. Items like one-shots and Session Zero have already been mentioned in the *Beginner's Guide to Role-Playing Games*, but I will go over how they'll look from your perspective when in charge of the game. You'll also receive some tips on streamlining your process to run your sessions as smoothly and efficiently as possible.

Tips and tricks can be helpful, but they're nothing without preparation. And I don't just mean laying out the character sheets, having your own dice tower, and putting out bowls of snacks. You'll need to know the basics of a TTRPG session and how to prepare for it as the person in charge of guiding your players' world. This means understanding the game's structure, knowing what to do when your tablemates go off script, deciding how to adjust your campaign on the fly, and much, much more.

Shaping your world like this is the core of being a Dungeon Master. Improvising dialogue, figuring out combat on the fly, and quickly adjusting your whole campaign story to fit one of your players' motivations are just a few of the things that will make you a great DM. My goal for this book? To give you the tools and knowledge needed to enjoy an RPG like *Dungeons & Dragons* from the perspective of a Dungeon Master while also teaching you how to run the game in a fun and exciting way that will keep your players coming back for more.

The role of a DM is simple in theory; you create a game that your players and you both enjoy. What does this mean? At its core, being a Dungeon Master relies heavily on imagination and flexibility. When a player throws a curveball your way, you have to be able to catch it and then throw it back at them, all while figuring out a way to get your players back on track. Being a DM is all about harnessing that creativity in order to have fun.

Chapter 1:
Learning the Basics

First, let's discuss terminology. The person in charge of running the game is usually called Game Master (GM), except if the game is *Dungeons & Dragons,* where the person in charge is called Dungeon Master (DM). While both are acceptable terms, some people like to get specific, so I will stick to saying 'DM' to minimize the confusion.

Fun fact: the term Dungeon Master does come from the term Game Master, as back in the early days of *Dungeons & Dragons*, many Game Masters had their own homemade levels, known in the community as 'dungeons,' and people would go to GMs in order to play that specific dungeon, hence Dungeon Master.

What We Learned So Far

First and foremost, how does a typical game of any TTRPG function?

The Dungeon Master sets the scene and gives players options on what they can do. Mainly due to the fact that a DM is human and can adapt on the fly, the players usually have an almost limitless number of things they can do. Whatever a player decides to do, they will convey that plan to the DM, who will determine their success based on a dice roll. Usually, a game will consist of three standard pillars of role-playing games: combat, role-playing, and exploration. Some people add a fourth pillar – puzzles – but this is fairly self-explanatory and is mainly covered in the first three pillars, so I won't go into too much detail about it.

What we care about in this guide is related to all three pillars. As I said, the role of the DM is to be a referee. What we need to keep in mind is that, despite referees usually being unpopular in every sport, in the world of TTRPGs, they're also a part of the game, and while this particular ref controls the game a lot more than, say, a basketball referee, they are still meant to have fun *with* the players.

Your role as the DM is to control the flow of the game, establish and maintain the rules, and be a key part of collaborative storytelling. Easy, right? Yeah, not always. As a rookie DM, you will face challenges, but don't worry - you will learn to overcome them.

My first-ever DMing experience was absolutely nothing like I had planned. What was going to be a meticulous campaign centered around rebellion and war slowly turned into a forbidden love story between two NPCs, which resulted in a surprising amount of investment from all of my players. The campaign took a comedic turn, and I found myself losing interest, which led to a less satisfying outcome. I was disappointed for a while, and I still feel that way at times. However, I've shifted my perspective, realizing it was more about how I handled the change. Now, I see it as a learning experience that helped me grow as a DM.

Being a first-time DM is hard. To me, it felt like my entire career as a DM was riding on whether or not that first campaign went well. It was hard to believe at the time, but as I grew more as a DM, I realized that that first campaign experience was the perfect first step in this new role I had. That campaign not going the way I had wanted was the best introduction to the world of DMing. My players were close friends of mine, and we all trusted each other and could laugh together; my mistakes and minor inconveniences were brushed off and overlooked by them. I was in a good environment to be a new Dungeon Master, and that campaign, the hilarious train wreck that it was, taught me immensely about the unpredictability of DMing.

That is why I look back on that campaign and feel a twinge of guilt about how I reacted to its unexpected twists. I learned a lot from that campaign; I shouldn't have let that feeling of failure bother me for as long as I did. Ever since that campaign, I've grown and developed my personal style of DMing, which is something that every dungeon master does as they grow. I'm sure you will develop your own style as well as time goes on.

Know the Rules Before You Break Them

This might be one of the most concrete pieces of advice on this list. Perhaps it seems a bit obvious, but I felt like it was important enough to add here. Every TTRPG has rules; whether it is a particular way of creating characters or a specific combat method, there are always some guidelines on how to play. These rules ensure every TTRPG feels unique, so when you switch games, you don't wonder, "How is this any different?"

As a newer DM, it is always good to have the rulebooks – if there are any – and any printouts or notes with explanations of said rules you need to help you with the campaign in front of you. As you grow with your players and as a DM, I think that you should always keep the core rules of the game close by as a reference, but you might find yourself altering some of the rules or making small edits as you and your players see fit to make the gaming experience more fun.

One great advantage of the digital age is that we no longer need to carry every rulebook to a session. Most rules and interpretations, especially for popular games like *Dungeons & Dragons*, are easily accessible online. If you're playing a more obscure game with hard-to-find rules, having a core rulebook can be helpful. But remember, as the DM, you have the freedom to make final rulings when needed!

However, knowing and understanding rules are two different things. This can sometimes lead to disagreements at the table as some players believe they know the rules better than the Dungeon Master. While that may be possible, you shouldn't be discouraged. Still, I feel this is the perfect time to mention the concept of RAW, RAI, and RAF.

RAW stands for 'Rules as Written,' and it's a way for a DM to establish among the players that they will make judgments as the rules are written in the book. While this is how most game designers intended their rules to be followed, it's also worth noting that sometimes the rules aren't clear for a specific situation that they didn't anticipate. Approaching the game rules in this way is how most beginner DMs do it, but it may not be the best approach for you.

In those situations, a DM might be forced to use **RAI**, which stands for 'Rules as Interpreted.' If you're doing things this way, you are opening yourself to possible resentment from the so-called 'Rule Lawyers,' but you're also giving yourself more flexibility when it comes to making a judgment. Once you've got the hang of being a DM, you will be better positioned to make fair decisions when dealing with a moment where the exact situation isn't perfectly defined.

The most rewarding part of being a DM, at least in my case, is using **RAF**. It stands for 'Rules as Fun,' and it's meant to encourage DMs to use their own interpretation of the rules in a way that adds fun and excitement for them and their group of players. This is a slippery slope, however, as it can lead to some uneven moments. Which, if you kept the game otherwise balanced and entertaining, shouldn't be an issue. In my experience, you should use RAF once you have mastered the rules and know how to keep your group roaring with laughter while having a satisfying gameplay experience.

There is, however, a somewhat unofficial way of looking at rules. It is called the **Rule of Cool,** and it is pretty similar to what RAF is. ROC ideology is pretty straightforward - if a player comes up with a cool idea to solve a problem, a DM should let them do it, even if it bends the rules a bit. Of course, there is a reasonable amount of rule-bending you should allow. If a player wants to throw a dagger at a dragon, you can't exactly have it hit the dragon in the eye and kill it in one shot. Or maybe you can. You are the DM, after all, and you make the final ruling.

Rules Shouldn't Overrule Your Gaming Experience

It is a bit amusing that I'm telling you not to let rules overrule your experience while being in the middle of giving you a bunch of rules. Alas, this 'rule' is here because I find that sometimes Dungeon Masters can place a heavy emphasis on the rules, and while that's fine, you can sometimes lose the spirit of the game within all of the rigid rules following. It is okay to manipulate rules to better the gaming experience. If there is a rule you and/or your players don't agree with or you find limiting, you can change it or take it out completely. At the end of the day, this is your game to play, and as long as everyone's on board and enjoying the game, you might as well make it work for you.

Now, when I say that rules shouldn't be the end-all, I'm only referring to the rules of the TTRPG you are playing. I'm not referring to the table rules; those should always be honored and respected. The goal of having rules is to create a fun, creative gaming experience. They are not there to ruin it, so it's okay to mend a rule or even a couple if all of your players have a better experience.

Set Your Table's Rules

Every table needs to have some semblance of rules or guidelines. Every TTRPG player and DM have different opinions about what is okay and what is not okay. Having a fun experience is all about setting boundaries and agreeing upon a set of table rules. While some tables are okay with more explicit gaming, others prefer PG gaming. Some tables allow phones, and others don't. It is really all up to you and your players. I know of some groups that don't mind drinking or smoking at the table, but I also know of some that don't allow one or the other or, in some cases, either.

Table rules should be created upon the creation of the group. If there is any disagreement around what people are okay with, see if compromises can be made. There should be no shame for anyone based on their comfort level, but there should also be a mutual understanding that all group members should feel safe and comfortable while gaming. This would mean that if 4 out of the 5 group members don't want to drink at the table, the remaining group member should either agree not to drink or should be assisted – kindly – with finding another alcohol-friendly group to play with. Table rules are there so that everyone is comfortable and everyone enjoys themselves; after all, that is what the TTRPG experience is about!

System-Oriented Approach to Running the Game

This book probably makes you think it's exclusively *D&D*-related, but I also want to give you some advice on how to run a game that differs a little bit from the standard high-fantasy of *Dungeons & Dragons*. Needless to say, *D&D* is the most approachable game and is a great game to start, but if you want to up your TTRPG experience, this section is for you. I will quickly go over how some other games (or systems, as they're sometimes called) take their approach to game mastering.

Pathfinder is essentially an offshoot of the third edition of *Dungeons & Dragons* and is, therefore, very similar to it. However, it is different from the versions of *D&D* that are currently the most popular in that it retains that old-school feel of heavy emphasis on mechanics. So, while the DM would have a similar role, they will be expected to know their rules a lot more and have stats for every encounter prepared well in advance.

On the other side of the coin, we have a system like **Fate** that is more of a way to play an RPG rather than give you specific rules you must follow. Here, the focus is more on storytelling and the Game Master collaborates more directly with the players in order to create an enjoyable story. The prep work you would have to do here is more focused on setting up broader themes than figuring out specific details of events or battles.

The Call of Cthulhu takes another approach to RPGs that I really appreciate. This system is very atmospheric, and the focus on mechanics like sanity is the key element the person in charge of running the game has to be aware of. So, in a sense, as the GM in this game, you're more in charge of setting the right feeling of horror and dread while paying attention to your players' actions and giving the right subtle clues.

Blades in the Dark is a fun system I particularly enjoy, but I rarely get the chance to run. It's a game that is dedicated to teamwork and places emphasis on players working together to choose how they go about their goals, giving the GM a more reactive role.

As a long-time **Star Wars** fan, I enjoyed the franchise's few relatively recent TTRPG forays, such as the **Edge of the Empire** and **Force and Destiny**. Both of these games have a unique narrative dice system, which makes the GM's role much closer to that of the referee while still giving them the freedom to put their own spin on how players' actions play out.

All of these systems bring their flavor to the world of tabletop role-playing games, but at their core, they are still role-playing games. This means that you can still do funny voices, improvise, and set unique challenges for your players – it's just a matter of knowing the rules before playing. It's that simple.

For most of these games, just like with most TTRPGs, there will be three core pillars in how the game is played, and it's just a matter of adjusting to the right system.

DM's Role in Three Core Pillars of TTRPGs

I previously mentioned the three core pillars of TTRPGs: combat, role-playing, and exploration, with some adding a fourth—puzzles. In this section, I'll guide you through how to approach your role as a DM within these essential aspects of gameplay.

Let's start off with **combat**. I feel like this is the most straightforward part of any game, so let's get it out of the way quickly. This part of the gameplay is mainly related to the game system you're using, which is why it's necessary to be familiar with rules and have good organizational skills to keep track of the events.

In the example of *Dungeons & Dragons*, you will have to keep track of the order in which players and their opponents take their turn. You should also have stat blocks for the enemies of your players, as well as a way to keep track of everybody's health points and other modifiers. Obviously, *D&D* is a bit more complicated than that, but as a beginner DM, that is the basics of what you need to pay attention to.

As the person in charge, you will be in charge of narrating the actions, rolling the dice, and checking whether or not the players or the monsters succeed or fail in their turn. Before getting to combat, you should also give your players context for it. Was it an ambush? How many opponents do they have? How many can they see? How much can they tell about their enemies' strength based on appearance?

Having an answer to these questions is a surefire way to becoming a better DM. The background of a battle, as well as its course, can help shape the whole experience, which is why you should have a good reason for entering combat. If you know *why* your players are battling certain enemies, you will know how to implement stuff like role-playing during combat or knowing how and when to push a particular player's agenda.

Combat can be a great tool for building tension and excitement, and it allows you to control the pacing of the game. However, combat encounters can sometimes drag on, so you may need to find ways to wrap them up more quickly when necessary.

Including a battle in your session isn't always necessary, especially when playing with newer players who may still be learning the ropes. In these situations, it can be helpful to guide them more actively and provide support. On the other hand, when playing with more experienced players, you can challenge them and see how resourceful they can be on their own.

If you wish to up your DMing game a bit, you can also utilize environmental effects on the combat. This can be stuff like giving a participant an advantage for having a higher ground, setting a useful hiding place for combatants who fight from range, or even mentioning a precariously balanced ornate chandelier that just happens to hang over a group of bad guys.

If you were to add these extra things, it would help you increase immersion for your players, and that is something you always want to do. Besides adding immersion, using the environment to your advantage can also help you control the pacing of the combat. Who's to say that dangling stalagmite won't fall off just at the right moment and create an immediate shift in the field of battle?

Of course, you should also keep in mind the spell effects your players have on them when entering the combat, or if they're at a low health. This sort of stuff is something that you will learn to keep in mind over time and through experience, but for now, it might be worth it to have a checklist before engaging your players in combat with NPCs.

And so, here's the list of things you need to pay attention to before and during combat:

1. Pre-existing environmental effects – you need to know the exact details of where the battle is taking place. If it's by a stream, you need to tell your players that, just as you would if it happened atop a wizard's tower. There might

be some things that aren't immediately available or noticeable to your players, and you need to approach them carefully. Either ask your players to roll the dice to see if their characters spot something or wait for them to ask themselves. Your choice.

2. Pre-existing combatants' conditions – before the battle, it's best to know where your players are health-wise. This gives you plenty of options to balance the encounter, especially if your players are low on health and you decide to go easy on them and give them a weaker enemy. Or, perhaps your players are hunting a group of enemies and have cornered them with nowhere to go. In that case, it makes sense that enemies are scared, weakened, and more prone to surrender.

3. Initiative – in *D&D*, as well as in many other games, the order in which players take their turns is determined by a dice roll called initiative. There are usually modifiers to that, but those can be system-specific or depend on other in-game conditions. Once the order is established, you can proceed with the combat.

4. Know who's fighting who – have your NPC stats prepared. You don't have to have the same for your players except for things that will influence combat, like their armor and health. Remember, despite being relatively rugged mechanically, the combat is still part of a role-playing game, and your players have a role to play. So, have your side of the combat figured out and allow your players to do their own moves the way they want to.

5. Make smart choices for NPCs – unless their Intelligence stats are in low single digits. Seriously, if your players are facing formidable foes, they will attack with the same ferocity and cunning as your players. That means stuff like using the environment to their advantage, thinking out their moves, or ganging up on a player. Of course, it isn't easy to keep a good grip on these things when you're just starting out, so remember to take things step-by-step, not be afraid to take things down a notch, and keep them simple.

6. Know what happens afterward – just like in real life, it's possible your players will just want to

smash something and will start a fight for no reason, but ideally, there would be sound reasoning behind the combat encounter. Make sure to have things prepared for the moment that comes after the battle is settled. If your players want to question an enemy or want a specific item from the boss, make sure you're ready for it.

Role-playing is often considered the heart of the genre, and for good reason—it's literally in the name. That said, I've been in plenty of games where people were the least interested in this aspect, and I've also played with groups that take role-playing to the extremes. We're talking not just funny voices but full-on costumes and even special effects. No matter where you land on the spectrum, it's important to acknowledge this part of gameplay.

You must be prepared to deal with all sorts of players. Knowing your audience is something that will be addressed in depth later on, but the way you go about role-playing is kind of dependent on that. So, if you have a bunch of shy people who mainly joined the group to have a power fantasy of slaying dragons with power swords, you may not want to put them in situations where they have to talk their way out of a predicament that might lead them to not want to play. On the other hand, if you're DMing for a bunch of theater kids, you may want to dial down the combat aspect and focus on giving them interesting roles to play.

Now, role-playing doesn't purely mean putting on funny accents when talking as your character – it also means that you have a role you play during the gameplay. As a DM, your role is basically every role that doesn't belong to your players - and that can be extremely difficult to pull off.

As a DM, you take the role of every NPC (non-player character) your party encounters, and it is your duty to give them the right feeling. Every NPC you present to your players should have its place in the story – be it an ordinary villager your players decided to bother for some extra fish they're going to use later to toss at armed guards or a story-important castle servant who can lead them down a series of secret tunnels from which they can assassinate the king's evil advisor.

Again, depending on your group, you will give and appropriately manifest these NPCs' characteristics. If your group doesn't feel like doing voices and play-acting, you shouldn't feel pressure to do it either. Just give general descriptions of what the NPC says and does and move on. Likewise, if your group is on the other end of that spectrum, you might want to carefully consider the personalities you're going to give each NPC and how you're going to act them out.

The vital thing to note here is that as a DM, you're also meant to have fun, which means that you should role-play only in the way you're comfortable with. This means giving a basic description of character actions if you're not into acting them out, but more importantly, discussing these preferences with your players during Session Zero.

The interesting thing about role-playing is that sometimes you will find yourself in a situation where your players want to interact with someone for whom you haven't been prepared. As a DM, it's your job to be ready for these sorts of situations, even if you are not anticipating them.

My honest advice would be to keep a stack of interchangeable NPCs with character histories, descriptions, motivations, voices, and everything that might make a good NPC. I'll go over how to keep these NPC files ready, but for now, you need to know that you have to be prepared to role-play, even if you don't always want to.

I'd like to emphasize what I believe is the most significant reason to role-play, and that is to advance your story and hook your players. While some people may be more into combat or solving puzzles, a lot of TTRPG players will form some sort of connection with their character and will want to help them accomplish their goals. Empathizing with characters is a core human emotion, and if you are able to get your players invested, you can share amazing stories with them through multiple sessions.

To this day, I remember a brilliant moment of inspiration that came to me while I was unexpectedly DMing for my standard group of players and one new player. I was forced to quickly create a backstory for him in order to give his character motivation, and while brainstorming, I had an idea to hook him immediately by having him interact with a group of villagers who spoke of a group of bandits who are for some reason looking for somebody looking like him. Luckily, the guy didn't take a hint, and as he joined the players, they conducted a full investigation only to understand when the final clue was revealed that the person of interest was him all along. He stopped the game to show me the chills he got, and I will always treasure that.

These little moments when you can show players that they can be important to the story are a sure way to get them coming back for more. In my example, this player, along with other players, went on an adventure to uncover a mystery and were practically put into a position where they had to interact with villagers to get the right information, and all of that led them to have a satisfying story.

That example does also tie into another element of TTRPGs – **exploration**. In order to further the story, my players went around and looked for clues, which led them to investigate physical aspects of the world besides interacting with villagers. In fact, that final scene where they figure out the bandits have been after one of them this whole time happens after they stumble upon their secret lair and are rummaging through their stuff.

For some groups, this can be the most engaging aspect of the game, and knowing when to lean into that is key. Some players will love exploring their surroundings just for the fun of it, while others might do it to push the story forward or gain an edge later on.

Making exploration accessible and encouraging not only gives players more agency but also offers you, the DM, some advantages. If you have done a substantial amount of worldbuilding, this is your chance to give your players a reason to care for your world. If you are crafty with your words and know how to create an immersive scene through narration, you can control the pacing and create a unique atmosphere during this section.

Let's face it: most people are into TTRPGs because of either combat or role-playing, and exploration is often overlooked and seen as a bridge between the two. However, I think that during the exploration phase of a session, you can create your most vivid hooks and give your players a reason to keep playing the campaign you're running.

My favorite part about the exploration segment is creating the atmosphere. Believe it or not, TTRPGs also have their genres and subgenres. For example, you can use exploration to create the atmosphere of a spy thriller by using the appropriate visual cues or background music. The right atmosphere is also a great way to further your storytelling, so make sure you take advantage of that if you want to improve that aspect of your DMing.

You can also use the atmosphere to handle pacing. After a particularly thrilling combat section, you might want to take some time to give your players and their characters a chance to rest mentally, and describing a relaxing walk by the stream could be just what you need. Or you may feel like your players and their characters are dragging their feet, so you decide to add some spooky elements to add a sense of urgency.

Handling exploration can also lead your players to new levels of creativity. If you do a good enough job as a DM in describing the environment, you may get your players an opportunity to engage their curiosity and try new things. This can then lead to opportunities for you to improvise and improve your DMing skills.

Now, let's talk **puzzles**. They have a special place in my heart because solving them was one of the biggest reasons why I got hooked on this genre. As with any part of TTRPG gameplay, there will always be players who don't enjoy it, and that's totally fine. However, as a DM, there are plenty of good reasons to include puzzles in your game.

First and foremost, puzzles are just plain fun. It's as simple as that. But there's more to it - puzzles can help the game flow better, with one of the biggest benefits being the teamwork they encourage. Even if your players are longtime friends, they might not know how to work together in-game if they're new to it. Using a puzzle to bring them together is a great way to foster teamwork and strengthen their desire to play as a group.

Just like exploration or role-playing, throwing a puzzle at your players can be a great way to increase immersion into your world. If you crafted your own world, this is a perfect opportunity to throw something at your players that will improve their knowledge of your world's lore and further the story while creating a sense of accomplishment.

Creating a well-balanced puzzle is a razor's edge, though. Sometimes, you will feel like you created a perfect puzzle that will create tension and excitement or provide an alternative solution to a combat encounter, only to have your players stumble and waste hours of real-time to solve it.

In a situation like that, you are put in a tough spot because you have essentially locked yourself in a puzzle. There is little wiggle room to change it as you already set the starting parameters, and your players will be dissatisfied if they aren't resolved. You can get around this by layering your puzzles. This means that you create several solutions that build upon each other, and then, depending on how efficiently and satisfyingly your players are going through them, pull a trigger and present them with a solution. Sure, this isn't ideal and may still lead to some player malcontent, but sometimes, they just can't solve what you envisioned, and you have to scramble to provide a proper resolution.

The number of times I had to quickly google puzzles for five-year-olds and the number of times my players still failed to solve them is way too high. Like, it's embarrassing. For me, for them, and quite frankly, for the five-year-olds. However, that doesn't mean that I will exclude this part of the game from the next time I DM. I will just learn how to make them better adjusted for my players.

That just might be among the best pieces of advice I can give you – keep learning from your mistakes and keep improving your DMing skills. I consider understanding these core pillars of the game a core skill in the DM skill tree, but the most important one is knowing that a role-playing game is a collaborative storytelling experience.

General Advice

I have plenty of advice in my sleeve; unfortunately, some of it just doesn't neatly fit into a group with the other, so let me give it to you rapid-fire style.

If You Expect This to Be Your Own Story, Turn away Now and Write a Book Instead

---

Okay, that might sound harsh, but unfortunately, the number of times I participated in a campaign where it was apparent the Dungeon Master just wanted to tell their story was way too high.

The DM isn't writing a campaign for themselves; they are writing a campaign for their players. This is their story, and as a DM, you are overseeing it. In a way, you really are the voice of some higher power, guiding them along but not entirely interfering with any of their decisions. TTRPGs have a significant emphasis on the free will of the players, and as long as the players are acting according to the table rules, they should be given that free will.

This rule can definitely be challenging, which is something I understand. Creating a whole world – NPCs, lore, villages and cities, and more – and giving it up to your players to interact with can be extremely nerve-wracking. I've met a couple of folks who didn't want to DM simply because they didn't want to create something and have it changed or meddled with by others. However, I find it exciting to world-build and create a universe for people to live in and enjoy. Being able to be the catalyst for the journey my friends get to go on is something that I find really cool. Perhaps you will feel the same way!

The best advice I can give is to think carefully about your goals before starting a TTRPG campaign. Maybe you've built an amazing world in your head, and perhaps you have some perfect stories that could unfold there. If that's the case, it might be worth sitting down and writing them out instead because, as much as we wish it were, time isn't an unlimited resource.

Work With Your Players, Not Against Them

If something isn't working, or if your players are questioning a rule or a move you made, you have to be able to communicate. Even outside the TTRPG realm, communication is extraordinarily valuable. There have been times when I have been DMing, and my players stopped me mid-combat to tell me that they thought the monster they were up against was at too high of a level for them. I double-checked the monster's stats, and yes, it was far too high of a level. Frankly, I felt a bit embarrassed about it. At the time, I did get somewhat defensive – something I regret now – and tried to play it off like I thought they could handle a higher-level monster between all of them. This was just not the case, though, and when I look back on that now, I wish that I had been more open to their concerns.

Every TTRPG is about enjoying your time playing, but not everyone is going to enjoy their time playing if they feel like something is unfair or off-putting. It is the duty of the dungeon master to be open to listening to the concerns of the players without judgment. I believe you should expect that same respect from your players as well. If you and your players work together to create the best gaming experience possible, then everyone at your table will be that much happier – including you.

Under-Planning Is Better Than Over-Planning

Typically, it is the other way around, but alas, everything is a bit strange in the world of TTRPGs. I tend to find that overplanning as a DM is a waste of time. Players rarely stay so on track and on time that you need to dip into your notes with extra information. Not only this but if your players go in a different direction than what you originally planned for that session, you are then stuck with a bunch of notes that aren't applicable for the next handful of sessions. From my own experience, this leads to frustration and feeling like you have wasted your time. Neither of those are very productive in the realm of TTRPGs.

This is another one of those scenarios where your ability to plan improves as time goes on. At first, I find most Dungeon Masters over-plan everything, and then as things progress, your DM is rolling up with a paper that only says rabid raccoon with a question mark at the end like they haven't even made their mind up about that one.

I know that as a beginner DM, you may feel like there is never enough information and you just constantly feel chronically under-prepared, but you will soon find out that that is what it means to be a DM. You will quickly learn to bottle those feelings up like the rest of us.

Of course, there is a specific way you plan just enough, but it is a bit of a balancing act – like most things are when trying to be a good Dungeon Master. Being knowledgeable of the world and the story you're trying to tell is the best foundation you can lay for yourself to be prepared for whatever your players might throw at you. As I mentioned earlier, keeping a stack of interchangeable NPCs ready to go is a great way to help yourself when you need to improvise in a tough spot.

Conclusion

These rules are obviously not set in stone or things you have to follow. They are here to offer some guidance towards starting your journey as a dungeon master. A lot of being a Dungeon Master is really just throwing yourself into it and figuring out what works for you and what your players enjoy doing. However, I will say that all of the previous advice can be very helpful for both new and old dungeon masters. There are many important components to being a Dungeon Master, and sometimes, it can be nice to have a list of helpful advice when you feel overwhelmed or forgetful. Most DMs keep a folder, binder, notebook, or a somewhat organized paper stack of information around when they are running a game so that that information can be easily accessible. Most of the time, this information is simply a part of the Dungeon Master's DMing station.

Chapter 2:
Setting Up

You may or may not feel like you are ready to run your own TTRPG session, and that is fine. I still have lots of tips and tricks for you, so make sure to keep up because, in this chapter, I will go over some basics, like what physical tools and materials you should have, as well as more advanced techniques, like collaborative character creation.

As with many things in life, you should prepare before being in charge of running a tabletop role-playing game. And yes, that does include being up to date with your game's rules (official or self-imposed) and knowing how to set up a game with a perfect hook. Let's get to it.

Importance of Understanding Your System

When playing any game - virtual, tabletop, or even sports - you should at least be partially familiar with the rules, especially since you will be acting as a referee and playing a pivotal role as a Dungeon Master.

As I mentioned earlier, it isn't necessary to know every single rule by heart. You *can* have a rulebook nearby for when you need to make a quick arbitration, but that is a nuanced statement, so let's dive deeper into it.

As a DM, you must have strong knowledge of game flow, especially if you're playing with newbie players because they will be looking to you for guidance. This may be a bit worrisome if the entire group, including you, is just starting to get into TTRPGs. However, *you* made a decision to run the game as a Dungeon Master, and that is your burden to bear, as unjust as it may be.

I'm dramatic, I know, but remember I'm a DM as well, and that is part of the job description. But it's not all bad, though, because, at some point, you'll figure out how to control your friends' actions as if they are the puppets and you are their almighty puppet master.

Regardless of your players' experience levels with these sorts of games, you are still the one in charge and *should* be the one who knows the rules the best. That is, of course, unless your party contains a DM's worst nightmare - a Rules Lawyer.

By definition, while a player who challenges your ruling is not necessarily a Rules Lawyer, more often than not, they are. To reiterate - a Rules Lawyer is someone who follows the printed rules to a T. This means looking at game rules as written and, often, exaggerating and using them in their favor.

A Rules Lawyer is a player-specific term in TTRPGs, and you shouldn't worry about being one in your role as a DM. You are in charge of making the final arbitration, meaning you decide what rules to follow and how closely. What's most important is making sure both you and your players are having fun.

You should also make sure you are as consistent as you can be with your rulings. If you were to, for example, determine that a player takes four points of damage for falling ten feet, you should stick to that scale for the rest of the game. As much as TTRPGs are less rigid than video games, players still like to have some semblance of order.

If you are aware of the rules in the first place, you will have an easier time handling somebody who challenges your ruling. What's important is establishing your authority as the ultimate judge of rules as soon as possible; otherwise, you may lose control of your game.

Controlling out-of-line players isn't the only reason to learn your game's rules; you also use those rules to run things more smoothly. Knowing how a session should flow rules-wise is a perfect foundation for running the story and characters in your world. If you know what is possible within the game's rules, you know how to tell stories, play out character arcs, and, most importantly, have a blast doing it.

If you have worldbuilding aspirations, learning the rules will allow you to make your world more logical, coherent, and, above all, playable.

Going even further, if you want to create custom rules (otherwise known as homebrewing), you will need to know the base rules before you can modify them. I'll touch upon homebrewing more later, but understanding how the game functions from top to bottom is the perfect starting place for adding your own personal flair.

Tools & Materials

As much as I've wanted to chuck a rubber eraser at my players at some points, that isn't the reason to bring one. Or maybe it is, to each their own. In either case, an eraser is one of many essential tools to have on hand when running a classic pen-and-paper RPG session.

Other tools and materials for this type of game include stuff like pencils, character sheets, battle maps, dice, and rulebooks. If you followed the last section, you already know that you need to have those things ready because you already know the rules and, thus, what is necessary to run a game.

To be a functional DM, you really only need three things: paper, a pencil, and some dice. Honestly, I know people can get very enthusiastic and buy dice trays, dice towers to roll their dice in, or dungeon tiles so that you can customize the game and make it more visual for your players. There are also miniatures that you can get for your characters and the monsters that they will face. Those are all awesome and, frankly, can be super fun to have around. However, I really want to stress that a good game of any TTRPG does not have to include anything fancy.

If you do want to get more into the expensive side of DMing, you could take a look at items like terrain, miniatures, dice trays, dice towers, and fancier DM screens. When Dungeon Masters bring terrain to their games, it creates a visual to help further immerse their players into the campaign they are playing. The same goes for miniatures.

They are figurines that can be used to emulate player characters, monsters, NPCs, and pretty much anything in the TTRPG realm. Typically, Dungeon Masters use them with terrain to show where everyone (the players, whoever they are fighting, NPCs, etc.) is on the battlefield. This helps players visualize who is around them, which in turn helps them make their combat decisions.

Dice trays are somewhat self-explanatory. These are used to cushion the roll of your dice and keep them contained in one spot so that you don't have to scramble awkwardly to get them all after they inevitably fly off the table and roll underneath the cabinet where you haven't cleaned in years, or worse yet right next to all your players atrocious smelling feet.

Dice towers are used to roll dice so that you don't have to. Most of them work the same; you drop a die into an opening, and the die rolls down a miniature spiral staircase, negating your need to hand-roll it yourself like a medieval peasant. They typically come with dice trays as well. They can take a bit longer to roll, but it negates any argument of anyone "dropping" their dice straight down instead of rolling them properly.

The Dungeon Master's screen is a physical block between you and your players. For some, it is a couple of cardboard panels that block eyesight, so players don't peek at any inside information. For others, it can be a hand-carved, intricately crafted wooden masterpiece that resembles castle walls. I once even used the pizza box from the pizza we finished minutes prior.

I've also met some who prop up their tablet or laptop and just get started. When I first started DMing, I looked up a tutorial on how to make my own DM screen, and for the first year of my Dungeon Master career, I had a DM screen I crafted from canvas panels and duct tape. I was the epitome of both style and function! That DM screen did the job somewhat well, proving you don't need expensive tools to be a Dungeon Master.

The DM screen is a multifunctional tool. While yes, it is used to block the eyesight of the players, Dungeon Masters also use it to carry additional information. Most DMs have rules of the game they are playing posted on the screen to prevent themselves from having to flip through a bunch of pages if they forget something. Imagine how cool you will look running a game for the first time and instantly knowing the answer to a newer player's question.

On my own DM screen, I make sure to have the basic rules for the TTRPG I'm playing, as well as some more tailored information based on the campaign I'm doing. It helps to have those right in my eyeballs, as it saves time when I'm having trouble remembering something. The only thing you should be careful of is piling so many notes onto your DM screen that it topples over during a final boss battle since you can't find that one thing you need and start frantically shuffling piled-up post-it notes around... I'm totally not speaking from experience...

To give you an idea of what a Dungeon Master screen might look like, I can try to describe how I set up mine. My current DM screen comprises four panels, each dedicated to a specific topic. It depends mainly on the TTRPG that I'm playing, but typically, I have one panel for the rules, another for things that I usually forget, and another for just the basics – it can be campaign-related or character-related, it depends on your preferences – and then one dedicated to the campaign I'm hosting.

On top of that, I typically have post-it notes reminding me of the different player characters and all of the extra things that I might need right in front of me when I'm running a campaign. Behind the DM screen, I have my dice tray, loads of dice, all my notes, and anything else I feel may be helpful during the campaign. If you keep it all together, it is pretty easy to remember to bring, especially if you are like me and have the memory of a goldfish.

The most important aspect of your DM screen is that how you use it is entirely up to you. I think it is absolutely brilliant when I see Dungeon Masters decorating their screens and making them their own visual masterpieces. The DM screen, in a way, is an extension of yourself as the DM, and it is valuable to view it as such. You can think of it as an extra brain or an extra pair of hands, as it can really work as such. Don't be afraid to get creative with it since your DM screen has the potential to be your favorite – and most helpful – tool that you bring to your table.

Of course, I mentioned earlier that some people use electronic tools such as tablets or laptops to help them DM, and that might be the perfect solution for you. Having a device like that, you can easily hop online and google any rule you might've forgotten. You can also organize your notes without dealing with a bunch of papers and even roll virtual dice. I personally like to use these auto rollers when I need to roll multiple dice of the same type.

The solutions offered here are mostly low-budget, but that doesn't mean you can't build your own custom gaming tables with dice trays, cup holders, and a built-in TV that serves as a virtual map. While that definitely would be an enjoyable experience to some, I still can't justify the cost to my wife... And I don't even have a wife.

Personally, I find it most immersive to have everything in physical form. Guiding a session that way can help you develop your skills as a DM because it encourages prep time, and the more you prepare, the better you're equipped to deal with unexpected situations.

And, oh boy, will those situations occur. But, in order to have them in the first place, you may want to have stories, settings, and characters crafted beforehand. And what if you're unsure where to start?

Creativity 101

Creativity can be one of the easiest or hardest things, depending on who you ask. Don't worry if it feels challenging for you now because I have your back.

Good news! Most TTRPGs have preset modules you can download designed to guide new DMs through the entire campaign, step-by-step. These modules typically include a wealth of worldbuilding details and characteristics for key NPCs, along with well-timed plot hooks. They also provide alternatives for handling situations when players inevitably wander off the path you've planned or choose not to engage.

A premade campaign like this is perfect if you want to test out a system and see if the game mechanics are a good fit for you and your party's personal style. Another reason to use these premade modules is as a simple, ready-made campaign to cut down on the prep work you need to do as a DM.

On the other hand, if you are a DM who needs to have every detail figured out before starting your campaign but isn't sure where to begin, I have good news for you.

Start Small: Growing a Mighty Oak From a Tiny Acorn

If the idea of creating a whole world seems overwhelming, that's okay because it's a big task, not to be taken lightly. Planning to create your own momentous world will inevitably give you questions on where to start, and my answer is - wherever you're the most interested.

I'm serious.

Even if you became interested in storytelling or worldbuilding by something obscure and seemingly unrelated, like the idea of a lighthouse in the middle of a desert, start there. Ask yourself the questions you think your players might ask to help set you on a path of creation. This helps slowly build your world, brick by brick.

Simply placing yourself in the shoes of someone living in your world - a player or an NPC - is often enough to kickstart your worldbuilding journey, and you'll quickly realize you don't need to know everything right from the start.

If you imagine yourself as an ordinary villager in your world, would you be intrigued to go and explore that lighthouse in the desert? Does the mystery give you enough to abandon everything you ever knew in pursuit of adventure? If the answer is yes, then you know where your next worldbuilding step should be - the desert and everything in it. Are your players going to attract mysterious sand dwellers who will attack them because their sacred land is being disrespected? You're the only one who knows the answer.

Good Artists Borrow; Great Artists Steal

Many newbie DMs feel that they have to create something entirely new and original, and that's just not true - stealing ideas from other mediums is perfectly fine. Some of the best campaigns take an old idea and breathe new life into it.

In other books in this series, I have mentioned something called Anxiety of Influence. In short, that means that a creative person is paralyzed by fear of accidentally creating something that is too similar to something that already exists. In this scenario, a creative person would want to create something and worry that their target audience - in this case, your players - would find it derivative.

Maybe you want to create a legendary, world-altering artifact, but you're worried it's too similar to the One Ring from *Lord of the Rings*. I understand where you're coming from. After all, I spent many years dealing with that same Anxiety of Influence, but I eventually found freedom.

How?

I just decided that I didn't care. Obviously, my journey took longer and had some twists and turns, but that's the gist of it. Even if you do intentionally base something on an existing piece of media, you still have enough creativity in you to add your own unique spin to it - and you should remember that.

In fact, you should lean into it.

Do you love the political intrigue of *Game of Thrones*? Take that as a starting point and build a kingdom rife with backstabbing nobles and squabbling, yet sometimes incestuous siblings. Was there a horror movie villain who really scared you? Borrow some of his traits, give them a few twists, and then let him loose in your world. Creativity doesn't mean reinventing the wheel. More often than not, it means taking what is familiar and tweaking it in a way that feels fresh and exciting for your players.

Take inspiration from wherever you'd like and rework it for your world. Do you love that creepy old mansion in that horror movie? Well, figure out how to fit it into your high-fantasy world! Maybe it's some sort of ancient tower where sorcerers from times forgotten dwell, or perhaps a castle from another kingdom as damned as the dark magic which spawned its birth. The point is - you need to rework those ideas you love so they don't stick out like sore thumbs against the tone of your campaign.

Remember, you are making a campaign for yourself and a few friends to enjoy. What's important is that it works well together and flows, not that you create it all yourself. Unless you are planning to publish your campaign somewhere, don't worry about theft of intellectual property or copyright; just worry about enjoying the time with your friends and building memories. You will end up straying from your notes and needing to improvise at some point anyway, so don't worry about who and what you copy; you and your players will make it your own as you play. Speaking of which...

Draw Inspiration from Your Players

Believe it or not, you are not the only one who can bring creativity to your world. If you pay close attention to your players' characters, backstories, and especially the things they're passionate about during gameplay, you can use that information to shape the world and create personal story arcs that resonate with them.

While you can't fully implement this approach during the initial stages of worldbuilding or campaign creation, it becomes a powerful tool as you adapt and refine the story during gameplay. Building these personal connections over time deepens your players' emotional investment, something worth prioritizing as your campaign unfolds.

A straightforward way to get creative ideas out of your players is just to ask them questions - about their character's hometowns or who the most influential figure in their character's life is. The more you know about your player's characters and their backstories, personalities, and other traits, the easier you can build a world collaboratively to create a setting that feels more dynamic and specific to your group.

Use Random Generators and Tables

More often than not, a random generator is a quick and great way to kickstart your creativity. You don't even have to riff off of it - you can just take whatever the random generator throws your way and go from there.

If you've played *Dungeons & Dragons*, you've likely encountered these tables. In order to simulate randomness, game systems will allow the DM or the players to roll dice and then consult the corresponding field in a table. This is a great way to use random effects in a game, but also a great way to create unique characters and places.

With the advent of the internet and computer technology in general, the need to do this in physical form has almost vanished. That's not to say that some people out there aren't still doing things the old-school way, but many newer-generation DMs prefer to use a computer tool rather than a piece of paper and dice.

Having these sorts of "random" tables a Google search away is a great tool to utilize in your DMing journey, especially if you want to make your job easier in the moment.

Focus on What's Fun

Just remember, creativity shouldn't be a grind - it's play. As I already mentioned, one of the best ways to approach the creative process in any given TTRPG is to focus on what excites you. If you're passionate about some kind of story, theme, or even location, bring that into your game. Your enthusiasm will be contagious, and your players will appreciate investing time in crafting a world that's got you excited.

For example, if you like horror tales, run with it. Creating macabre, blood-curdling environments in which your players can discover all sorts of dark secrets is a blast. If you're into epic fantasy, build high cities and sprawling kingdoms full of political intrigue and daring adventure. The key here is to pay attention to what inspires *you* rather than to try to adhere to one style or another.

Your creativity will continue to grow when you allow yourself the freedom to explore ideas that genuinely interest you. Rather than forcing yourself onto the things you "should" do, create what gets you most excited to DM your next session.

One-shot or Campaign

Approaching your first time as a Dungeon Master can be incredibly overwhelming, even if you have a whole world prepared and stories in it lined up. For this reason, I, and many veteran DMs like myself, like to recommend running a one-shot first.

If you are a relatively new DM, which I assume you are, I suggest that you run a one-shot first because that way, you don't have to focus on stuff like worldbuilding or campaign planning. I understand that you might feel like you are capable of running a full-time, years-long, level one-to-twenty sprawling campaign, and I won't discourage you from doing it eventually, but I will encourage you to wait until you've run a one-shot first.

The reason is simple - if you run your first campaign by following a formula, you'll get a first-hand experience of what a session looks like while also having contingency plans set out for you in case of an emergency. Such as your players deciding they want to eat the talking goat who came in begging for help, thus eliminating your main plan for getting them necessary information. And if I had a nickel for everytime this happened to me, I would have two nickels, which isn't a lot but it's weird that it's happened twice.

When gathering the necessary experience by grinding out (DMing) a few low-level quests (one-shot sessions), you'll be ready to level up and that full-time, years-long, level one-to-twenty sprawling campaign you always wanted to.

Basics of a One-Shot

Sometimes, I find the title of "one-shot" a bit misleading because it doesn't fully capture the variety these sessions can offer. A one-shot can span a single session, a handful of sessions, or even extend beyond that. One-shots aren't always just a "one-time" experience. I have even had one-shots develop into a full-fledged campaign when my players have fallen in love with the characters and world set up. So, I once again encourage you to start with a one-shot first and work your way up to the grand vision you may have.

There is a multitude of reasons why people decide to play a one-shot over a full-length campaign. They can be used as a break from a campaign or a way to introduce the game to new people (or for a new DM to dip their toes into the DMing waters!).

They can also become full-length campaigns if the DM and players all want to continue with them. See, while campaigns are typically indefinite in their length as they can last for months to years - I've been running the same campaign with one of my groups for the last five years - one-shots have more of a definite timeline.

They can be as long as you want, but there is always an end in sight when you play a one-shot. Typically, one-shots are planned from beginning to end, meaning there is always a general goal that your players should accomplish. The main campaign style I suggest to newer Dungeon Masters is one-shots precisely because of this aspect. When deciding how to go about a one-shot, the most important thing to keep in mind is that because it is just a shorter, more limited campaign you can essentially try whatever you'd like. If you mess up, it is okay! If you try something and don't like it, that's fine. It is all about your own self-discovery and enjoying this new adventure with your friends. But to begin with, feel free to keep it simple.

Benefits of Running a One-Shot

You can use one-shots to try new things and experiment with different NPCs, campaign styles, and more. They are an excellent way to figure out what works for you best as a Dungeon Master. They also give the players a chance to work with other characters they have less experience with or don't want to commit to long term.

One-shots are often used as a learning experience, so it is best not to take them super seriously for your first time as a player and a DM! It is a learning experience for you as well as for your players, who may be new to the game, their character, or the mechanics being used. It is best to keep track of what you like and don't like. You can also ask the players what they enjoyed and what they didn't enjoy, thus being able to better yourself as a DM.

A one-shot campaign is a great way to get feedback on what your players enjoyed. It can be beneficial to run a one-shot when you are playing with a new group or have a new player. They are also great for less of a time commitment when you just want to get together for a few hours on a Saturday once or twice a month to hang out and play. There is really no limit to what a one-shot can be, and I hope that, due to this, you take advantage of the absolute insanity of running a one-shot.

If you are less of a beginner - say you have played a couple of times or DMed a campaign or two – it might be fun to use a one-shot to try different rules or test out different story concepts just to see what you can get away with and what you find fun. I think that people unconsciously or unknowingly try to put a limit on what one-shots can be when, in reality, it just means different things to different people. In my opinion, one-shots are limitless in what you can do, and I find them very freeing and less stressful than a long campaign.

What Kind of One-Shot Should I Use?

There are three main one-shot styles that I find people use the most. They are as follows:

1. Premade one-shots
2. Custom one-shots
3. One-shots that tie in with your current campaign

Just to quickly recap - premade one-shots are usually officially-made mini campaigns you can easily follow along to hone your DMing skills. These one-shots can also be made by almost anybody, but the core idea for us is they're ideal for beginners.

More often than not, though, these premade one-shots from an unofficial source (like your friend, a random person on the internet, or even you) are called custom one-shots. Of course, there are other names for it, such as homebrew, but that's just semantics.

When it comes to one-shots that tie into your ongoing campaign, I recommend doing them only once you've practiced your DMing skills because they are more challenging since they connect to an already existing storyline.

If you're interested in incorporating a one-shot into your current campaign, there are multiple ways of doing this, such as creating a prequel for your main characters before they meet, a side adventure featuring minor characters that players might want to explore, or a one-shot set in the same world that subtly influences the main storyline. These approaches allow you to expand the world and add depth without overwhelming new Dungeon Masters like yourself.

Premade one-shots are definitely the easiest. Everything is there for you, ready to go. Most of the time, they include everything you'll need to tell the story, like the ideas for your player's characters, locations such as cities and surrounding villages, and the NPCs that will exist in the world. You can feel free to add in a few personal touches (I almost always do), but if you prefer not to, everything is already there for you.

When creating your own one-shot, you have to take everything into account: the location you want your players to be at, the NPCs that they might meet, the villages your players are going to be at, the central conflict, the plot, and everything else in between.

However, since it is just a one-shot, you could always just pull everything right out of your... hat. Trust me – you could very easily just roll a die and see what it lands on and go from there. That is the fun of running a custom one-shot! You don't need to get as involved as you would with a homebrewed campaign.

The beauty of a custom one-shot is that you can create it by taking a premade one and picking it apart. Don't like that the setting is high up in the mountains? Send it down to the beautiful coastline with sandy beaches, cocktails, and attractive half-na... Wait, what was I on about?

Anyway, you can customize premade one-shots as much as you want; just be prepared for a possible 'Ship of Theseus' moment where you replace too many parts and have to wonder if it's the same one-shot anymore. As in, there's going to be a point when the official premade one-shot is less that and more of a custom one-shot. Neither point on that scale is bad, though; it's just that some people prefer familiarity.

One-shots are fantastic ways for both you and your players to familiarize yourselves with a new game, so be sure to make good use of them. But remember - just because things are laid out for you, that doesn't mean you shouldn't prepare. And one of the most important prep tasks is knowing how to structure a session before it even gets started.

Structuring a Session

Having a clear sense of how a session might unfold is valuable for any DM, not just beginners. If you can perfectly predict how a session will go, that is on par with clairvoyance, and if you already have that trick in your pocket - just go and buy a lottery ticket.

Not knowing what will happen isn't the end of the world. This is why we prepare in advance, establishing a preferred structure for the session - even though, inevitably, players may take things in an entirely unexpected direction. That's just how the cookie crumbles - or, in this case, how the dice roll.

We'll delve into the art of navigating unexpected twists soon, but first, let's lay a solid foundation by exploring the core elements that breathe life into a truly memorable session. These essentials are the heartbeat of your game, setting the stage for everything that follows.

The Hook

Whether watching a movie, playing a video game, or reading a book, something drew you in that made you continue engaging with it. It may have been a fantastical location, the central conflicts, or just seeing Sydney Sweeney and Henry Cavill as leads. Also, sorry, but that movie doesn't actually exist. And if you have no idea who those people are, it doesn't matter - all you need to know is they are hot and popular. My point is that *something* made you feel like you can't miss out. These "somethings" are often referred to as a 'hook.'

In the TTRPG world, hooks are pretty simple. You are often already operating under the assumption that everyone has a rough idea of the setting and the genre, but the hook is what really brings players in and makes them want to play the game.

When determining the hook for your session, first consider the scope. Is this a one-shot that you can reasonably wrap up in one session? Is it likely to spill over into the next one? Are you running a session that may turn into or relate to a longer campaign?

Knowing the answer to these is often the best place to start. As a new DM, I recommend choosing a relatively simple story hook. Something that you can easily follow and know how to give a satisfying ending to.

A simple hook could be a rescue mission, a treasure hunt, or the investigation of a weird cult. Don't worry about being a bit predictable; it's your first campaign, after all, and turning a predictable hook into an engaging story isn't difficult. There is a reason why troupes exist; it's because they work and are effective. You don't need to reinvent the wheel to have an entertaining game, especially as a first-time DM. Once you have your hook, you will start to develop plans for handling the rest of the session. Let me first give you some pointers on choosing a great hook.

As a DM, you want your players to be interested in whatever story you have crafted, and that means that you have to start with something they are able to grasp and understand. You can't just tell your players 'begin' and expect them to know where to go and what to do.

When writing a story, you'll often hear the advice to start "in medias res" - right in the midst of an important event - to immediately captivate your audience. While that approach works wonders in traditional storytelling, remember that as a DM, you're not here just to tell *your* story. Instead, your role is to shape the story *with* your players, creating an experience that unfolds through their choices and actions.

Starting out, you may want to give your players a peaceful place where they can get acquainted with the location and characters before throwing the hook right in their face. No, Mike Tyson, I said throw the "hook right in their face," not "throw a right hook in their face," if you want to throw things at your players, try the eraser idea from earlier... or throw snacks... everyone likes snacks.

A good example of doing this would be to start your players in a tavern. Now, if you have any experience at all with TTRPGs like *D&D* before, you know this is an extremely common trope, but for good reason. A tavern atmosphere will be something that you, as a beginner DM, will be able to easily explain because you can easily equate it to a modern coffee shop or bar atmosphere. On top of this, starting in a tavern gives you an excellent opportunity to deliver your hook. Plenty of characters frequent taverns; you can put virtually anyone you want in there.

You can have a child enter looking for their missing parents, a treasure hunter searching for muscle to pillage an ancient castle, or your players simply overhearing a group of worried locals loudly talking about some mysterious shenanigans that are taking place around town. All of these help set the scene quickly while giving players immediate knowledge of what's in store for them.

When creating the hook, remember to use it to give your players clear and precise goals to keep them intrigued. Doing so will provide your players with the motivation to embark on their own adventure but will also give you a rough idea of where that adventure is going.

The (Optional) Twist

A good story also has a good twist- something that changes the perspective of the story unexpectedly. After revealing the initial hook, your players will probably have a pretty good idea of where the story is going. That is, of course, unless you surprise them with an epic twist.

As you could have guessed from the title, a twist isn't something you need every time. I would even go as far as to recommend you not have one for your first few sessions - just so you can get in your DMing groove before trying this somewhat advanced technique. Still, it's good to know how structuring a twist works in structuring the whole session.

So, what makes a good twist?

We've all seen movies or TV shows in which some new information changed the whole story. It could've been something like a character who was portrayed as good being revealed as bad (and vice versa) or the protagonist receiving new information that changed his motivation. As the word implies, it is something that twists the story.

The best part about it is that it can be used effectively in collaborative storytelling.

A twist is most effectively utilized once players settle into a groove and are moving at a steady pace to solve the overall conflict. Throwing in a twist should make them adjust that pace but also the path they're on. Be careful about how you twist your story - you want it to be something that adds intrigue and makes the players want to keep going. A lousy twist has the potential to derail the whole campaign. When I talked about hooks, I mentioned setting them up to be intriguing yet clear so that your players will want to resolve them. This also means that you should keep those in mind when adding a twist. You don't want your players going all, "What the hell is even that?" and losing interest in the whole session. You want them to gasp, look around nervously in shock and awe, and question their entire existence knowing they'll be unable to eat, drink, or sleep until they have solved this mystery.

Plot twists can be the seasoning that turns a good campaign into a truly unforgettable one - when done well. But when they fall flat? They're the sour note in an otherwise well-composed symphony. Disney's twist villains are a perfect case study for understanding what works and what doesn't. They're widely recognizable, making them relatable examples, and they demonstrate a spectrum of success, from masterful to downright *bad*.

Some Disney twist villains are infamous not for their cleverness but for their inconsistency or predictability (spoiler alert, I guess?). Take Hans from *Frozen*. He's set up as a positive character throughout the entire film. Even when he's alone, he continues to act selflessly, which makes no sense for a character who's supposedly manipulating everyone for power. Why would he keep the charade going when there's no one around to fool? His betrayal feels less like a shocking twist and more like a slapdash decision made to spice up the ending.

Another example is Assistant Mayor Bellwether, the sheep from *Zootopia*, who had a twist so obvious it felt more like a straight line. Every "bad guy" in the movie we see working with Nighthowlers are a type of sheep, and Bellwether is constantly shown being bullied or dismissed by the more socially powerful "preadtors" in her life. It's not a leap to guess she'd snap and turn out to be the antagonist. Predictability kills tension, and a good twist thrives on subtle, clever foreshadowing—not flashing neon signs.

Finally, we have Professor Callaghan from *Big Hero 6*, who might be most frustrating because his twist outright betrays the character's established personality. He begins as a caring mentor, only to lose all humanity over his daughter's death. This descent might've been believable if properly set up, but instead, we're expected to accept that this formerly good man burns down a building, gets a student (who was trying to save *his* life) killed, and shrugs it off with, "That was his mistake." To make matters worse, the movie teases a fake villain - CEO of Krei Tech, Alistair Krei -who's so over-the-top suspicious that it practically screams, "This isn't the real bad guy!" It's as if the writers decided halfway through production to shoehorn in a twist, completely butchering Callaghan's character in the process.

What do these examples teach us? A bad twist often fails because it's inconsistent, obvious, or feels forced. Crafting a satisfying twist starts with intention, which means you can't just decide on a whim to throw in a shocking reveal and hope it sticks. Twists work best when they're planned from the very beginning and woven seamlessly into the story with consistent foreshadowing. When players look back, they should have an "aha!" moment, recognizing the clues you planted, rather than feeling blindsided by something that came out of nowhere.

Consistency is also critical. Your characters need to stay true to their established personalities and motivations. If a sudden twist forces a beloved NPC or villain to behave in ways that don't align with how they've been portrayed, it breaks the immersion and makes the twist feel forced. Players thrive on narrative cohesion - they should be able to understand why a character made a surprising choice, even if it catches them off guard in the moment.

Finally, subtlety is your best friend. A twist loses its power if it's too obvious. If your players can predict the outcome long before the reveal, the sense of surprise is gone. Foreshadow just enough to give your twist depth and credibility without telegraphing it too clearly. A twist should feel like uncovering a hidden truth, not spotting an oncoming train. And above all, make sure the twist serves the story rather than derailing it for the sake of shock value.

If you're looking for an example of a good twist, check out *Wreck-It Ralph*. I won't spoil anything for you, but the clues are all there, the twist is consistent with the story, and it adds depth without derailing the plot. If you want to learn more about crafting intricate twists, be sure to check out our next book on becoming an expert Dungeon Master. It picks up where this one leaves off and covers more advanced techniques, such as the aforementioned twists, creating and running lengthy campaigns, and crafting NPCs from scratch that are memorable and have logical story arcs. But for now, remember: a poorly executed twist can derail an otherwise great story. Learn from Disney's missteps, and you'll be well on your way to running campaigns with plot twists your players will talk about for years.

No matter how and if you do a twist, you have to reach the...

The Resolution (Climax)

After capturing your players' interest, you can guide them steadily toward the campaign's climax. In this case, you do so by building tension and upping the stakes until you throw a final battle or a big reveal at your players and have them all gasping and applauding your genius while you're taking your gracious bows.

Typically, you'll resolve the question that initially hooked your players, ensuring the answer makes sense and fits naturally with the course of the session.

Remember a potential hook I mentioned earlier of a crying kid leading your players on a quest to find his parents? Well, you're not going to have that kid drag your players to the woods to save his parents and then throw a cocktail party in the middle of the forest honoring the marriage of a princess and a distant ally of the king. No, you're going to get your players to woods and then have them find the kid's parents tied to a tree, after which they will have to fight off a nasty cult who planned on sacrificing the parents to their deity. Once that is done, the kid has found his parents, everyone is safe and sound, and who knows, maybe now is the time for that cocktail party. A pleasant resolution, wouldn't you say?

You might feel that setting up hooks and reaching a suitable resolution are two distinct points in time with a lot left unexplained in between - and you're right. But that sweet spot is what makes these sorts of games thrilling.

Try to imagine your session as an art class. You're a professor who gets to help his students (players) create a masterpiece (a beautiful painting), but you can't paint the whole thing yourself. Instead, you can only occasionally use a big brush to give them an idea of what they can do. You see, you're an experienced artist and you painted something like this a bunch of times, but you can't paint it for them; only guide them to painting it themselves.

Just don't be alarmed if you find yourself chucking swaths of paint and notice that your players are drawing inappropriate stick figures, gluing googly eyes, or just writing profanities all over your canvas because they think it's funny. You will simply have to accept that *that* is your painting. Don't be sad that it didn't work out the way you envisioned it; the uniqueness is what makes it a masterpiece and googly eyes are cool.

In the next chapter, we'll dive deeper into handling the finer details of running a session, moving smoothly from point A (the hook) to point Z (the climax). But since we're here to cover the essentials of being a DM, I have to mention structuring of a session that's part of a longer campaign.

Seriously, though - and I can't stress this enough - start with a one-shot. I know you picked up this book to learn how to be a DM, and yes, that means you want to learn how to run a full campaign. But diving into one right away? That's just asking for trouble. You'll run into burnout and unexpected chaos and probably question your life choices as a DM at least once. Do yourself a favor: start with a one-shot, build up your confidence, and save that epic campaign for when you've got a little bit of experience under your belt... seriously - and if you decide you are cool enough to run a full campaign right now anyway and aren't going to listen (because that's usually how I decide to do things) don't blame me when your campaign blows up in your face, and your players make you cry... If you only listen to one thing in this entire book, trust me on this, it will NOT go well.

Your Regularly Scheduled Session

While running a one-shot is akin to watching a movie, having a long-running campaign is similar to running a season of a show. Sure, one-shots can stretch over multiple sessions, but that's like a movie series, and while some of those end on a cliffhanger (yes, *Empire Strikes Back*, I'm looking at you), which leaves the audience wanting more, most are considered separate entities. There is probably no better example of this than the *Fast & Furious* series. At this point, it may as well be a bunch of one-shots played by the same group of friends over the years. And given how Vin Diesel is a certified *D&D* nerd, I wouldn't put it past him to have done this purposely.

If my bachelor's degrees in Theater Arts and Film Production have taught me anything (and no, I am not bragging; if anything, I am crying out for help), there are different approaches to writing a movie script versus a script for an episode of a TV show. The same is true for a TTRPG session. If your central plot was built to be resolved in a single session, your hooks and climaxes would be paced differently than if you had a central conflict spanning a vast number of sessions in a long-running campaign.

But of course, these long-running campaigns still need to have a smaller conflict that is resolved each week, just like each episode of a TV show. So what if I told you that you could use the structure of a one-shot we just went over for each weekly session of that longer campaign? I am hoping you finally see why I *really* think you should start your DM journey by running a one-shot.

Whether you're running a one-shot or part of a bigger campaign, you'll still want a hook to pull players into each session. The difference is that a one-shot hook is a one-time setup, while the hook for an ongoing campaign session connects directly to the resolution of the previous session.

For a longer campaign, that means that the last time you played, you didn't directly resolve the last session's plot hook but rather twisted it in a way that satisfied your players and left them with unanswered questions for which they crave answers. One of the best ways to change a resolution to a twist is to utilize the "Yes, and/No, but" principle - which is a famous improvisation technique.

The idea behind its origins is that you want to keep the sketch going, or in this case, create a longer story, by adding a twist that modifies it. Seeing as you are telling this story with your players through multiple sessions, using this method of twisting is perfect.

Basic improv states that you pose a question and then answer it with a 'yes' or 'no' while adding something that happens directly afterward. The same is applied to a long-running TTRPG campaign. At the beginning of each session, you pose a question, and by the end of it, you answer it while changing your players' perception of the question in the first place.

This improvisation technique comes at the end when they have either accomplished their mission, and now a whole situation has arisen out of their actions, or they have failed their task, but there is an additional effect that makes it harder or modifies it.

Let me give you an example.

Let's say your players wanted to save the princess from the tallest tower of the highest castle that's guarded by a dragon. Yes, I recently rewatched *Shrek*. Why do you ask? Anyway, regardless of how your players end this conflict, you will have an opportunity to leave them on a cliffhanger you can resolve the following week.

In this example, you can say that your players *were* successful in saving the princess, *and* now they have to escort her back to the wannabe king who sent them on this quest. And, if they *weren't* successful, you could say that they failed, *but* now the dragon has decided to join forces with them as long as they keep away from the princess.

When you run a longer campaign, your players may see a twist ending from a mile away, which makes them less effective. For this reason, you may want to set up act breaks. In scriptwriting, an act break is a dramatic turning point that clues in the audience that one segment of the show is ending and the other one is beginning. In the world of TTRPGs, your players are both the audience (that wants to witness a good story) and the performers (that want to take part in a good story).

And yes, in this scenario, you are both the scriptwriter and the director, and in order to have a show worth watching, or rather, a campaign worth playing, you need to have a good opening hook. This means a hook that will intrigue your players to even start the campaign with you.

This starting conflict should set the stage for your campaign, giving players a reason to dive in. Ideally, it's resolved by the end of the first act rather than dragging on until the campaign's end, as some longer ones span years, which can cause players to lose interest... Don't ask me how I know.

An "act break" might seem tricky to apply in a collaborative game, but it can still be a powerful tool for structuring long campaigns.

By linking several one-shot adventures together, you can build a larger, continuous story. This allows players to keep developing their characters and progressing in the game, while also providing natural pauses in the story. These breaks don't mean stopping play, like when a TV show goes on a hiatus, but instead, give players a chance to celebrate small victories on their journey toward the bigger goal.

Let me give you an example from my favorite piece of fiction, which I hope you're familiar with - *Avatar: The Last Airbender*.

In the opening episode, we're introduced to Aang, someone with tremendous potential and ability to change the world. And the world is in *desperate* need of change, which is why it's his mission to restore balance to the world, so it's not like he can disappear. Again.

Early on, we are given the exact steps Aang needs to follow in order to save the world - something you can also do in your campaign. By the end of the first season (first act), he learns how to control water, which is a key step in him figuring out how to manipulate all four elements. And then, when the second season ends (or the second act), he knows how to manipulate earth and is now ready for the final step (act three) fire. By the end of the show, he has successfully mastered all four elements (he was a master of air bending prior to season one) and saves the world.

Incorporating a similar structure to your large campaign can also help you set up individual sessions. I'm not saying you should try to recreate *Avatar: The Last Airbender*, but you can use its thematic structure as a guide for the goals of your plot.

Let's say you want to run a world-saving plot. In the opening, you can establish a goal players will need to reach to complete their quest, and you can either resolve it at the very end or build upon it using the "Yes, and/No, but" method at the end of the first act.

Whichever way you decide to structure the overall plot, remember that players *need* achievable goals. These can be several sessions long or more contained, like solving one issue in one session.

When structuring a session for a long campaign, it's important to keep both yourself and your players grounded in the overarching plot while weaving in smaller, self-contained stories that push the larger narrative forward. These smaller hooks will help you keep your players... hooked... as you scale the mountain of your larger plot.

Once you have all the physical material prepared and fully understand your world, your plot and its hooks, and the rules of the game, you are ready to invite players and begin playing.

But, oh... What's that?

Bah, that's Session Zero's music!

Session Zero

Session Zero is a precious tool for all Dungeon Masters, not just newbies. It's not just an important session for one-shots; it's equally valuable - if not more so - when planning a full-length campaign.

The core idea of Session Zero is that you would spend around half an hour or even up to a few hours discussing your campaign. It is not a requirement, but it is an invaluable tool (so as far as your first campaign goes, it is a requirement.) It will help you to roughly present the genre and vibe of a game you want to run - something that will help your players understand how to set their expectations.

During this chat you should also be sure to highlight important stuff like table etiquette - and no, I don't mean if your players are utilizing proper utensils or not. I'm talking about things like how you will handle when players miss a session, whether or not food and drinks are allowed during a session, or how violently you will blow your lid if they pull out their phones to scroll Instagram while you're narrating. If you're anything like me, the answer is sky-high.

Dealing with player behavior is its own beast, so I will be covering it later in detail, but Session Zero is a time to talk about what you'd like your players to act like in an ideal world and also gives your players a chance to tell you what would be their ideal world.

Some DMs don't like Session Zero. There are some Dungeon Masters who make Session Zero a part of the beginning of the first session or some that even skip it altogether, but you'll probably want to keep things slow for your first campaign and dedicate plenty of time. If you really hate Session Zero, just skip it or shorten it for your second campaign; you won't know until you try.

However, like I said earlier, I actually really enjoy it. Being able to establish expectations with your players, for both you and them, is something that will create an environment where everyone feels heard and validated. Session Zero can – and should – be utilized to allow you as a Dungeon Master to make sure that your players are all on the same page and that all of the rules are communicated so that there aren't any possibilities of hurt feelings or people being made uncomfortable in the future. This is doubly true if it is your first time assuming the role of a DM.

The last thing you want as a DM is for any of your players to feel uncomfortable about anything that goes on at your table, in-game or out of game. It is your job as a Dungeon Master to ensure the comfort of all of your players and to leave communication open between you and your players. Make sure your party members feel safe and comfortable bringing things up to you either in the moment or afterward in private.

Do your best as a DM to assure your players that you are receptive to these concerns and handle them as gracefully as possible. Apologize if you make a mistake that makes someone uncomfortable, and gently point out to your other players if they make one. Remember, role-playing does not automatically equal consent; be sure your players are aware of this as well. These tips are incredibly important, especially if you are meeting some of your players for the first time. Not everyone is comfortable with the same things, and *D&D* and your table are supposed to be a fun and safe space. Please don't forget that.

Now that the important stuff is out of the way, Session Zero can also be used as a sort of Q&A for new players as well as a Q&A for experienced players who just want to further immerse themselves in the world you are building.

I often use Session Zero to help my players create their characters if they want assistance. This is useful both if it is their first time playing and if they need practical assistance or to be sure their character fits in the world I've crafted. A lot of my players like to get the "okay" from me before we start to play or like to use this creation process to feed me some extra backstory about their characters that I am able to fit into the campaign. Newer players may not have a backstory set up for their characters, so encourage them to make one (but remember that it is up to you whether you include it in the campaign or not, so don't feel any unnecessary pressure.)

Honestly, it is just super nice to just get together with your players before actually beginning a campaign. It helps people get excited for what is coming next, and if they don't know each other, it helps them get to know each other and gives them the opportunity to collaborate before being thrown into the lion's den.

Speaking of helping your players to create characters, you may also want to subtly nudge them in the right direction to make sure the party is balanced. Sure, a party of five bards and a paladin would be hilarious, but is it going to make for a satisfying gameplay experience?

Alignments are another balancing mechanism, and although primarily associated with *Dungeons & Dragons*, the concept of alignments influencing how you play a character can be applied to almost any RPG. In essence, they boil down to a set of traits or a moral compass that guides a character's decisions and actions. Understanding these traits can make it easier to step into a character's mindset, but not all alignments are created equal when it comes to fostering a smooth and enjoyable game experience, especially for newer players and Dungeon Masters.

In general, alignments are a combination of two axes: lawful/chaotic and good/evil, where lawful characters adhere to rules, structure, or a personal code, and chaotic characters value freedom, unpredictability, or personal desires. On the other hand, characters with one of the good alignments aim to help others or uphold moral virtues, while characters with an evil alignment seek to harm, manipulate, or achieve selfish goals at others' expense. Neutral characters, whether lawful, chaotic, or morally neutral, fall somewhere in between. Each alignment offers unique role-playing opportunities, but they also present challenges, especially in a group setting where teamwork and collaborative storytelling are key.

Some alignments, like lawful good or chaotic good, tend to align naturally with cooperative play, making them more approachable for beginners. These characters usually prioritize helping others or maintaining harmony, which supports the group dynamic. Neutral alignments, while more complex, can also work well, provided the player uses their character's neutrality to explore interesting dilemmas rather than derail the story. On the other hand, alignments like chaotic neutral or chaotic evil often pose significant challenges. These alignments can tempt players to act impulsively or disruptively, which might create conflict at the table or derail the game's narrative.

For newer DMs, I strongly recommend setting boundaries around alignment choices, particularly barring chaotic evil characters. While this alignment can be compelling in the hands of an experienced role-player, it often leads to actions that alienate other players or contradict the cooperative spirit of most campaigns. Instead, encourage alignments that promote teamwork and thoughtful engagement with the story. This approach not only makes your job as a DM easier but also creates a more rewarding experience for everyone involved. By starting with alignments that are easier to manage, you build a solid foundation for players to experiment with more complex characters as they grow in confidence and experience.

Venturing too far with experimentation may be too complex for new DMs, so err on the side of caution to ensure you don't overdo it. Still, even if you want to avoid combat, it's still worthwhile to learn the rules of it anyway because it will give you insight into how the game functions at a larger scale.

This conversation you have with your players serves as a great establishing shot of what your campaign is going to look like. You may want to keep some spoilers to yourself that you can use as a twist later on, but you should also be fair and tell your players what sort of campaign they can expect, at least at a base level. If they came in with the idea of playing a high-fantasy adventure, you might want to let them know if you're instead planning to run a gothic horror campaign. This gives them the chance to adjust their characters, mindsets, and expectations accordingly.

Something important to keep in mind is the potentially sensitive nature of collaborative storytelling. As a DM, you are in charge, and it wouldn't be nice to present a story that might be triggering to some of your players. It is a tricky topic to broach but it may be better to get it over with in Session Zero rather than having someone abandon your game because they didn't like the content.

As stated before, role-playing does not automatically equal consent. As fun as it is to have your bard running around "seducing" everything in sight, make sure all parties present are okay with this aspect, especially if it is *their* character being "seduced".

Similarly, as a DM, you may want to take your story to an incredibly dark and realistic place as you describe what happens to your players who just got captured by the evil, power-hungry ruler. That is okay in theory, but only if your entire party is also enjoying it. The darker and more risque a subject, the more important it is to check in with your players first to be sure everyone is consenting and enjoying the subject. The last thing you want to do is be putting your heart and soul into the gory details of a story that ends up negatively affecting one of your players' mental states. It will ruin the session, your hard work, and possibly even a friendship. But don't worry; everything will be fine if you check in with your players.

I also like to use Session Zero to utter a rather obnoxious quote, "In TTRPGs, the DM is usually considered a mix of a referee and a god. That is not the case here because I am a god and nothing else."

I heard your eyes rolling, don't worry. And I have seen the disgusted looks on new players when I say these words. I'm immune to death stares. The reason why I say this is so that I can run the game as smoothly and as efficiently as possible without every ruling being questioned and the flow of the game being interrupted every five minutes by a know-it-all player.

Now, I only say this when I'm running a *D&D* game for new players because chances are I know the rules a lot better than they do. I mean, I am writing this book, I ought to know something about it, don't you think?

As a new DM, Session Zero is something that will let you go over the official rules with the players, as well as your own personal rules. The best thing about it is that it doesn't have to be a separate day from the first session you play - you can just meld the two. Sure, the day might last longer with you getting to do less role-playing overall, but if you're playing with experienced players and only want to hint at the vibe of the campaign, you might as well get it over with in half an hour and enjoy a nice gaming session.

That being said, you may also end up on the opposite end of the time scale. Maybe you intended to make Session Zero take a full two to three hours, but you got everything covered in less than an hour. Sometimes, you may have already decided to have your first session some other day *after* Session Zero, giving you a chance to implement the valuable feedback just given by your players. If that's your plan, I suggest you bring something like a board game, so you have something to do with your group, just in case you end early.

I recommend you approach Session Zero as if you were a boxing referee. Obviously, the boxers know not to punch below the belt, but the ref still goes over the rules while encouraging them to have a nice, clean fight. You can do the same for your game session - present the genre or the vibe of the campaign, disclose specific rules you would prefer strictly followed, and make sure everybody is comfortable with the overall idea.

Conclusion

Okay, now you're ready to play.

Right?

Well, yes, actually you are. Dont worry. Session Zero won't run in swinging a steel chair. You can finally relax, take the time you need, and begin crafting your first session.

However, I want to give you a quick summary and a checklist you should make sure you have in order before running your first game. If this is your first time being a DM, though, I strongly advise you to use this as an *actual* checklist. Like, tick off the boxes with your favorite writing instrument (if you're reading this in a physical format, at least - I'm not responsible if you get purple sharpie all over your Kindle).

- **Know Your System**
  - ☐ Knowing how gameplay works
  - ☐ Having a rule book nearby (just in case)
- **Physical prep** (jumping jacks; they only increase real-world "Athletics" skill)
  - ☐ Character sheets
  - ☐ Pencils
  - ☐ Paper
  - ☐ Dice
  - ☐ Dice tower/tray (optional)
  - ☐ DM Screen
  - ☐ Combat grid
  - ☐ Minis (optional)
- **Session Structure**
  - ☐ Hook
  - ☐ Twist (optional)
  - ☐ Resolution
- **Session Zero**
  - ☐ Ground rules
  - ☐ Consent

☐ Campaign expectations

☐ Establishing your dominance (optional)

Chapter 3:
Running the Game

Five of your players are around the table. All on time, all brought snacks, drinks, and their own custom dice. You distribute the character sheets, check the notes behind your DM screen, and ask your players, "Are you ready?"

They nod their heads, and you ask yourself, are *you* ready? Panicked, you think, "No!" but it's too late. Your players are staring at you with buzzing anticipation. Sweat drops start forming on your forehead as you look at their eager faces. You have no idea what will happen now.

But why do you feel this way?

You prepared diligently!

Well, you may have done prep work, and while that is commendable, you may still lack the experience to actually be in charge of a game. But don't worry; this is *not* one of those things you can only learn through playing. Keep reading, and I'll teach you everything you need to be ready.

To run a session, you need to know the usual flow of a game, which I mentioned earlier. But, to quickly recap:

The DM sets the scene - through your narration and description of the environment players are in, they will get clues for the genre, vibe, and story they can expect. By giving them proper descriptions of the location they're in, you're also creating a sense of place, which is something they can explore. In this section, you also place your NPCs in the world, giving players someone to talk to.

The players tell you what they want to do - and you decide whether they succeed based on game mechanics. They might want to investigate something physically or talk to someone, and it's up to you to provide that experience. By responding to your players, you are essentially doing step one again, albeit on a smaller scale. This creates a loop that can go on until you reach a point where your players enter combat - or other similarly well-defined mechanical parts of gameplay. But after this segment is done, you're back to step one. Rinse and repeat.

Sure, there's a lot more to it, especially on the mechanical side, but for now, let's get more in-depth about telling our story.

Marching to the (Story) Beat

In the previous chapter, I introduced the concept of 'the hook' and 'the resolution' as points A and Z, respectively. And now I reveal to you that to tell a good story, you may add as many points in between as you'd like. You can even use the whole English alphabet. Go for the full Chinese one if that's what you want. But no numbers! They are evil.

If you have ever told a story, you know there were multiple exciting points, twists, and turns that kept your listener interested. The same concept applies to telling a TTRPG story - whether within a single session or spread out over multiple sessions. These specific points of interest are called story "beats," and they serve the purpose of tying a narrative together to make it coherent.

Now, as a DM, you are responsible for gently nudging players from point A to point Z, and using story beats is an excellent way to keep yourself, as well as them, on track. And the best way to accomplish this is to have a good idea of what your story beats are. In theory, this means you need those beats planned in advance, but they aren't even a must-have; they're more of a nice-to-have.

If you have your beats laid out in a neat little point A, point B, point C, and point D order, you should take one last proud look at them before your players toss them in a blender. In reality, they will likely go from point A to point e5 to point π to point $\sqrt{-1}$. Don't worry; this happens to everyone at one point or another, so try to have thick skin and don't let it become a big deal.

Of course, you may encounter players who diligently follow your beats, proceeding to have an adventure just as you imagined it. And if *your* players do this, please tell me what portal you pulled them out of and in which magical fairyland I can find my own.

A far more likelier scenario is that you'll have to wrangle your players like cattle just to get them to stay on track. In fact, it's possible you might even ask yourself why you're even trying to hook your players and get them back on track. If you carefully planned your session, you might want to keep fighting the good fight, but you also might be inclined to put your hands up and let your players follow whichever story they want to follow.

Railroading vs. Sandbox

I'm sure you know what a railroad is, but do you know the connection between that and role-playing campaigns?

Imagine you and your players driving a car and the story you have planned as a road trip. Your starting point is the hook, and your destination is the resolution, with a few stops sprinkled in, which I defined as story beats.

"How does that clarify the term railroading," you ask, and, "Well, both are transportation options," I answer. Hidden beneath the humor is my request for your patience.

You see, if your session is defined as getting from point A to point B (or C, D, E, and all the way to Z), then you have to have a method of transport. And if you're in a car, that implies you have the freedom to take a back road, get lost, slaughter a band of goblins, stop for gas, or whatever you like to do on a good road trip. But, if you are on a train track, your only option is to sit inside and observe your surroundings.

As a DM, you might find yourself panicked if your players opt to take a car instead of your train to reach the resolution of your session, and that's normal. You don't know what they're going to do, where they're going to go, or how long it's going to take them to get there. That's why your first instinct might be to switch from nudging them in the right direction to outright shoving them.

The idea of stonewalling, or refusing to communicate or cooperate with your players if they try to do something *other* than follow your story, might not sound the best, but there are situations where you might want to do exactly that.

Some excitable players might assume that everything you describe is some sort of a story hook or a twist that they're meant to investigate further when, in fact, you just got carried away and started describing a bountiful feast because you're staring at your players scarfing down pizza that you only have time to sneak small bites of (even though you're the one who paid for it) because you're being a good DM and narrating the story. There are other situations where players might be legitimately drawn to something interesting that you have plans on exploring.

In some instances, you might want to railroad your players because you haven't sufficiently prepared for possibilities outside your main story, and that's okay, too. In fact, there's a relatively clever way of keeping your players going in the direction you want them to, and that's known as the 'illusion of choice.'

Illusion of Choice

When you play a video game or read a choose-your-own-adventure novel, you may not be aware that the choices you make are pre-determined. On an intellectual level, you *know* there's a limited amount of options you can get, but when you're immersed in the story, you don't really think about it.

The same thing happens when you're on the other side, and you're the one crafting the story, as well as possible choices. You can't *really* anticipate every wacky decision your players make, so you use something called Illusion of Choice.

In essence, you will give your players the same story you had in mind, regardless of the choice they make. You're actually going to go a step further and *pretend* like they had a choice in the first place.

You see, you can present your players with multiple choices and then just go with whatever you wanted them to choose in the first place. Let's say they have an option of visiting one of three towns, aptly named Towneh, Townbee, and Towncee. The events you have planned happen at Townbee, but they choose to go to Towncee, and well, wouldn't you know it, those events now happen at Towncee.

What you did in that situation *is* trickery; have no doubts about it, but that's why it's called an illusion of choice. This is the most crucial tool in your toolbox if you want to keep your players on a railroad while giving them a satisfying session during which they feel like they are in charge.

Building Sandcastles or Eating Sand - the Choice is Yours

As you could've guessed from the title of this subsection, the opposite end of the spectrum is giving your players a sandbox and letting them play in it however they want. Not literally, of course. Sand is coarse and rough and irritating, and it gets everywhere, and who wants to deal with that?

The sandbox style of gameplay is really popular in the video gaming world, with the best example of it being a game like Minecraft. You're given this world with the ability to go wherever you want, and do whatever you want, and it's up to you to make your own fun. While it is possible to have this type of gameplay in a TTRPG, you will rarely use it as a beginner. Still, you should know what it is and how it functions.

In theory, you would know everything about the world and tell your players to go wild. This requires that you have either created the world and everything within it yourself or have spent a *really* long time studying somebody else's. Or maybe you're a *Star Wars* fanatic and already have the knowledge, so now you can role-play in a galaxy far far away, a long time ago.

Of course, you can also present your world as a sandbox-style adventure while performing the aforementioned 'Illusion of Choice' trick to tell a story you actually want to tell.

While both railroading and sandboxing are valid DMing styles, I still believe that TTRPGs are all about having a shared experience, which also happens to be *fun*. For you, your players, hell, even your cat can join in. Just don't let her near the sandbox.

So, if you want to tell a good story while also having your players follow along and contribute, you need to know how to *gently* nudge them in the right direction.

Wink, Wink, Nudge, Nudge (in the Right Direction)

You have your hooks, and your story beats, and you know exactly how you want this campaign to end. What you don't know is how to get your goldfish brain attention span players to actually follow along and get there.

What we talked about so far are some radical ways of controlling the narrative, but here, I want to give you a few hints on how you can keep players on track - besides the already mentioned 'Illusion of Choice' trick.

Say your players have just started their journey. They have a mission, they're invested in resolving it, *and* they even have a clue about where to start.

However, they have just started a campaign, are new to the world, and want to see if there's something *more*.

If you grew up without easy internet access (like some geriatric 30-somethings), you've likely had to blindly feel your way around a new game. I still remember my neighbor Mike down the street telling me of a 10-coin block hidden as a plain brick block and me running around levels bashing my skull into everything in sight until I found it. Oh, the exhilaration. But that wasn't the end - I continued banging Mario's head throughout the game in hopes of finding that treasure again.

An issue arises when your players look at you like you're a Mario level and they're the Mustachioed Italian plumber, and they keep going around the environments you narrated and, figuratively (sometimes literally, too), smashing their heads to find hidden treasures. Seeing how you likely made your world to be more complex than that, you might find yourself a tad offended.

But don't fret - you can always improvise a way to keep them on their path.

Maybe the particular town person they wanted to randomly talk to is mute. Perhaps they get frightened and run away, conveniently disappearing in an alleyway or blending in with the crowd. Or maybe they just give vague information, convey general disinterest, and refuse to waste time on talking to players.

What if your players are particularly interested in exploring the map?

Well, in that case, you could always learn how to draw a physical map. Want to know how? If you want to learn how to draw physical maps for your campaigns, we have a whole book on it - and it's free! It's called *The Advanced RPG Cartography Guide,* and it teaches everyone how to draw maps, even if they're a beginner DM struggling to draw stick figures. It will also teach you how to draw any location, step-by-step, from a river that flows through the valley to the fishing docks on its shores and even the village where the fishermen came from.

All you have to do to get this amazing book is scan the QR code and sign up for our email list! It's that simple! We will send it to you as soon  as you confirm your signup which will also have you receiving news and updates on any future projects we release! (We give things away for free all the time! And who doesn't like free?)

Thank you for taking the time to support our team! Being able to write RPG guidebooks is a dream come true for all of us and we couldn't do it without you! But that's enough of that; back to our regularly scheduled programming...

If you do decide to create your custom map, make sure to be deliberate about its contents because your players are very likely to have the attention span of a goldfish. So, don't draw anything on the map that might distract them. But if you're not using a map and your players *still* want to keep wandering around town, there are plenty of other solutions.

While you could resort to using a deus ex machina and simply telling your players that, poof, they fainted and are back where they started, that might just shift their interest to finding out how they fainted and teleported, which puts you in an even worse predicament getting them back on task. No, what you want to do is subtly hint that their physical surroundings are uninteresting - aside from the specific location needed for their quest, of course.

You can do this in a variety of ways; you just have to be creative about it. It's challenging to steer players away from a direction they're set on without making them even more determined to go that way.

A neat trick would be to use difficult weather or terrain. "Oh, you want to go that overlook half a mile east? Yeah, there's a sudden snowstorm. You can't really move that fast. You'll freeze before you reach it."

Obviously, you would do it more subtly, but you catch my (snow) drift. You could also pull something less subtle, like telling your players there's an impenetrable invisible wall stopping them from going somewhere, like when you reach the edge of the map in a video game - but that will probably make them more interested in finding out *why* they're unable to pass this invisible barrier. Remember, they don't think you have limits and will want to test you.

Even if your players fixate on an object or whatever else might be distracting to them, you should find a way to make it uninteresting in a way that will tell them indirectly that they shouldn't focus on that and get back to their quest. You can also flip this and use it to your advantage.

You can use something I mentioned earlier where players are at the crossroads of Towneh, Townbee, and Towncee, except adapt it to items. If your players are interested in a trinket, you may want to see how you can take advantage. They like a shiny ring that a beggar is wearing and just won't let go? Well, wouldn't you know it, now it's an essential quest item.

These are some subtle hints you can throw your players' way to remind them to keep moving and stay focused on the task at hand. However, it's also possible that your players *still* won't get the hint, in which case you have a bit of an issue on your hands.

Don't worry - it's nothing too serious.

So far, I've given you advice on how to gently (and not so gently) move players according to your script. However, you should know that sometimes it is okay to let them go off-script. You may not feel ready to handle going off-script because you obviously prepared a fairly rigid session, but with some ideas on how (and when) to improvise and adapt, you'll feel ready to keep your game fun *and* running smoothly in no time even when your plan goes awry.

Improvisation and Adaptability

In the previous chapter, I mentioned the "Yes, and/No, but" improv technique, and here is where you actually apply it how it was meant to be applied. If you can't get your players to move in the right direction, you may be forced to improvise, adapt, and overcome.

Using that improv technique is a great way to keep the pace moving, even when your players do something unexpected. The only issue might arise when you're unsure how to do that while keeping the pace and intrigue going. This will come naturally to you with experience, but let me give you a few pointers for now.

Using random tables or stacks of NPC cards can help you out if you're unsure what to do.

Keeping a list of random encounters, traps, magic items, puzzles, or treasures is a great way to kick-start a stalling session - especially when your players are refusing to follow your story beats and bite on your hooks.

The best thing about planning a session and having story beats is that you can use random events to get your players back on track. This idea only works if you're still clinging to your story, but if you feel that's no longer possible, maybe it's time to adapt.

Shifting a story on the spot is challenging, so I recommend adapting to your players between sessions - when possible. Especially when running a one-shot, there might be a moment during your session where you realize that your players have abandoned all interest in the story you laid out for them and want to chase magical fairies and their dust, so you'll *have* to make small changes.

This is difficult to pull off mechanically, but it might also be hard to do on a personal level. I mean, you poured your heart and soul into creating this story, this world, these characters, and your players are just not interested? That's rough, buddy.

Depending on the timing of your decision to adapt by improvising, you may toss different things at your players. If you realized right off the get-go that they weren't vibing with what you're serving, you might want to stage a more prolonged encounter that you have prepared in advance.

In the *Advanced RPG Cartography Guide* I mentioned earlier, I dedicate some time to a five-room dungeon model, which I highly recommend you use in an instance like this. The core idea is simple and, with enough prep time, allows you to have a satisfying session. Remember, join our email list, get your free copy, and read all about it!

On the flip side, if it took you the whole session to reach a realization that your players aren't catching your vibe, you might want to lean back on "Yes, and/No, but" and do something on a smaller scale that will shift the story and point them in a direction they might be more interested in. Maybe an NPC shows up who has a peculiar fishing rod and wants your players to help him fish. In this case, you and the NPC have something in common - you're both throwing hooks.

Be aware doing things this way can limit your options after the session is over. You might've wanted to take the story in the direction of a large-scale civil war, but due to tweaking something, your players are now interested in mushroom foraging, and you have to find a way to make it part of the main story.

While it's not always ideal that you can't execute the war story you've planned right now, look on the bright side - now you have a good idea of what your players are into for next time, and more often than not, that knowledge is worth the slight delay in your plans. After all, once you get through that period of mushroom foraging, you can often pick back up with some semblance of your original plan and head back to that civil war story you spent so much time on.

It all boils down to being aware of your players wants and knowing when to let them wander versus when to push them back on track. A skill you will further hone as you continue your DMing journey.

Of course, improvisation and adaption aren't directly related to just the story. Perhaps your players aren't happy with your combat-heavy style of DMing. Maybe they prefer a character-driven mystery more. No matter the situation, adapting is key to keeping the game enjoyable for everyone, and having an open conversation with your players is the best way to achieve this. Ask them what changes they want to see, and then try your best to implement them - it's that simple.

Also, if your players are losing focus or appear bored, that doesn't necessarily mean they've lost all interest - as illogical as that sounds. Sometimes, they just need a simple change of pace, and the best way to do so is to use the in-game mechanics.

Using In-Game Utilities to Control the Pace

You might remember that I talked earlier about how knowing the game system and its rules is essential; let me expand on that here. While knowing how a particular game session might start is vital, it is doubly important to understand those rules while you're running the game. And not just because you're supposed to be part-referee.

As a DM, you are a source of guidance for both the mechanical and narrative parts of the game, but what your players don't know is that you can use either to influence the other. Before I elaborate, let just put a disclaimer here that I will give direct examples related to *Dungeons & Dragons* as that is the most popular TTRPG out there, and you're highly likely to know its rules, which will allow you to follow along more easily.

So, in *D&D,* like most other RPGs, you set the scene for your players before they tell you what they want to do. But what happens when your players waste time on the boring stuff, like tavern brawling, instead of chasing the multi-layered political intrigue?

Well, you can do what I said in the last section and improvise and adapt if you think they're uninterested, but you can also keep the pace going by using gameplay mechanics.

Say your players are stuck at a puzzle, and it's really wearing down their real-life mood. Sometimes, you can "help" them by having them roll a dice to pass a skill check to get a hint. You can also provide them with a friendly NPC who just happens to have found a perfect hint lying around that your players missed.

On the flip side, if your players are just whizzing through encounters by either skill or luck, and you feel like they should have a more demanding challenge to fully appreciate the story's gravity, you can always modify your encounters on the fly by increasing the difficulty.

Your players are going through the guards like a hot knife through butter? Well, now the next set of guards has a pet dragon. They're solving the puzzles with ridiculously good rolls? Well, let's see how they solve the next one while they're fighting a dragon. They've been able to extract delicate information from any NPC they encounter? You guessed it - dragons.

A simple way to control the pace is by creating side-quests. These are missions that, as the name suggests, aren't as important as the main one, but can serve to fill in the time or provide additional context to the story.

A friendly NPC who follows your players around can be used as your literal in-game voice. Maybe that particular NPC is the exact reason why your players are on the quest they are, and he can make them go faster or slower, depending on what you think is necessary.

As is always the case in storytelling, the perfect way to control the pacing is to introduce a time bomb. Not a literal one, of course, but one used as a story device. This is something like your players needing to save the princess before she's executed for treason. Or maybe there's an invasion of an enemy army coming that only your players know about, and they must warn the king in time so they can prepare a defense. Maybe it's an actual time bomb within your world that will release some sort of poison gas and kill everyone in the world. Maybe it's Dragons... Time Dragons.

One way or another, you have tools to control the pace of your session, but how you use them is entirely up to you. The important thing to remember is that you have to keep your players engaged, and if they aren't, you might have pacing issues. One way to combat these is by offering rewards for completed quests. These shiny objects can keep your players' attention *while* helping with pacing - just be sure those rewards match the level of risk taken.

Balancing Risk and Reward

Balancing risk and reward is about adding just the right amount of tension so your players are on the edge of their seats but not so much that they start dreading every decision. You want to create a world where their choices carry weight, and the potential rewards make it all worthwhile.

I like to stick to the idea that if the players take a risk, it should mean something. Let's say they decide to charge a fortress full of bandits with no plan - maybe it backfires, and they lose a valuable ally or run out of healing potions for the next fight. On the flip side, if they spend extra time strategizing and making allies, show them it was worth it. Perhaps they avoid a trap or get a clue about the bandit leader's weakness that makes the next fight easier.

The key is to let their choices echo throughout the story. If players feel like what they do has a lasting impact, they're more likely to engage deeply with the story, even if things do go sideways. And sometimes, letting them fail can be as memorable (and motivating) as any victory.

Using a reward system might seem condescending, but it is still a great tool to keep your players motivated. Personally, I like to use certain valuable items after players accomplish a goal. I've used it so much that I pretty much Pavlov'd my players into going after side quests because they know they will get something memorable that will make the rest of the campaign more fun.

You don't have to use this exact method, of course, but using rewards is a great way to keep your players engaged.

Rewards are also a great way to keep yourself entertained. And yes, I'm making the puppet master analogy again. But these games are supposed to be fun for everyone - you included, so why not DM a game for your enjoyment?

If you are, say, someone who enjoys creative combat, you can make it so that your players are rewarded if they try wielding a smaller party member as a mace and using them against enemies - and no, of course I never did that... I made them put on a spiky helmet first.

As I'm sure you've figured out by now, RPG stands for *role-playing* game, which is why you might be inclined to reward your players if they get into character. This is a slippery slope if you have a shy player who isn't into role-play, though, because it creates a double standard they can't live up to. To skirt around these issues, you can choose to encourage character development. Just because you or I enjoy doing voices doesn't mean every player will, so be sure to *encourage* them, not force them.

A perfect mechanical way of rewarding your players is handing out experience points because they can be used to improve their characters - just like in video games. In fact, some players might even prefer to get their rewards *exclusively* in experience points.

Balancing risk and reward is a part of what makes the game feel alive. You want your players to sweat a little, celebrate a lot, and feel like every move they make actually matters. Give them tough choices and let them win big, but also let them fail and show them that even their mistakes add something valuable to the story. With a well-balanced sense of challenge and reward, you're not just running a game - you're creating a story that everyone will be excited to tell anytime someone mentions role-playing games.

I understand that, at this junction, it might feel challenging to figure out the perfect balance between risk and reward, but believe it or not, that's not the hardest part of running a session; the hardest part is real-life social encounters.

Encouraging Roleplay and Engagement

If you played *Dungeons & Dragons*, you may be familiar with its mechanic of encouraging players to role-play their characters - inspiration. In *D&D*, a DM can decide to give an inspiration point (that lets someone roll an extra die) to a player when they make an 'inspired' decision. It could be a smart idea they had that surprised you or you could just reward them when they are headed in the right direction so they know to "keep going that way." This extra die is called "advantage" and gives players a better chance of succeeding on an important roll. This is done at DM's discretion, so don't feel like you have to justify your decision to anyone, but remember to try to keep the same standards the entire campaign.

There's also a piece of good advice I have for you that applies not only to DMing but also to the real world - read the room. If your players aren't role-playing, it may be because your style is unfamiliar to them, or it could be they are shy and don't want to role-play at all.

You should discuss role-playing comfort levels at Session Zero so you know what to expect from your players, especially if you never played with them before. Still, some people may claim to be comfortable with role-playing when they are actually overestimating themselves. Or, the two of you could have different definitions of the term. Maybe to them, role-playing is saying things as their character would say them, but to you, it is doing intricate accents and acting out NPC actions. This is why player communication is essential, especially at Session Zero, but throughout the game in its entirety - even more so if your one-shot spans multiple sessions.

Sometimes, a player might be overshadowed by another player, causing them to lose interest in role-playing. As a DM, it is your duty to be diligent in these situations and point your attention directly at them. You might want to inquire what their character is doing and initiate an interaction between them and an NPC to reignite their interest.

You might also run into a situation where only one player doesn't want to engage, but that doesn't mean things have to be awkward. When I find myself in such a predicament, I try to role-play instead of the player, and I don't phone it in either. I try to show them how their character might act, and if I do a good enough job, I feel like they'd be more inclined to join in. Or they might feel like I'm not doing their character justice, so they decide to step up. Believe it or not, I've had the shyest players come out of their shells and become the most entertaining role-players due to pure spite after that exact situation played out.

To engage players in gameplay, you have to find what they like to do, what motivates them to play, and what makes them tick as players. Sometimes, they might just not be interested in role-playing, in which case I suggest you consult the previous section about giving players mechanical motivation to keep going. A cool combat encounter, fancy trinket, or just a good feeling of being a hero - this is about escapism, and you should allow your players to feel comfortable playing.

How To Conclude a Session (and a Chapter)

Knowing when and how to end a session is a skill that can elevate a game from good to unforgettable. The final moments of a session set the stage for what comes next, building either closure or anticipation.

When wrapping up one-shot sessions, the ending should provide a satisfying resolution within the limited time frame. The adventure arc is compact and needs to feel complete by the time everyone leaves the table. Aim to tie up loose ends by revisiting characters, plot points, or themes introduced earlier in the story.

Players should feel they've accomplished something significant, whether that's rescuing a town in peril, uncovering a hidden truth, or thwarting the plans of a dark villain. Shining a light on first-session foreshadowing, giving crucial NPCs dramatic comebacks, and overarching plot resolutions give players a sense of completion and victory.

This conclusion should be meaningful and clear-cut so players feel they've experienced a complete journey.

The best endings for one-shots are ones that leave players with that warm fuzzy feeling of accomplishment - satisfaction that comes from knowing they've done something impactful within the confines of the session.

However, if your story isn't self-contained like in a one-shot, you can use cliffhangers. They can be an invaluable storytelling tool to end a campaign session because they tease what's to come and keep players eagerly awaiting the next session.

This might involve a shocking plot twist, such as a betrayal by a trusted ally or the unexpected appearance of a powerful foe. The beauty of a cliffhanger is that it feels natural to the progression of the story while strategically building suspense. Players don't know how the current situation will resolve, encouraging them to reflect, speculate, and brainstorm plans before the next session.

An effective cliffhanger isn't just about leaving players in suspense; it's also about deepening their engagement with the story. By making the last scene both suspenseful and meaningful to their goals, you create an atmosphere of heightened anticipation that can carry over between sessions.

Ending a session well is an art of balancing satisfaction with suspense. Even when ending sessions of longer campaigns - where cliffhangers are the goal - providing players with minor achievements or rewarding discoveries will make the cliffhanger feel more impactful.

For instance, if the party hasn't completed their mission, perhaps they found a crucial clue, made a valuable ally, or acquired an item that promises to help them later. These small victories act as stepping stones, giving players a sense of progression while the story remains open-ended. If every session ends with some form of achievement, players will feel their choices have mattered, creating a foundation of accomplishment that builds with each successive session.

This balance between unresolved tension and incremental rewards keeps players engaged and invested over the long term, eager to see what the next step in their adventure will bring.

Recap
In this chapter, you've uncovered the core strategies and techniques needed to run a dynamic and

memorable game. From crafting engaging story beats to managing the balance between railroading and sandbox play, to utilizing in-game tools that adjust pacing, you're now equipped to create a session that is not only immersive but also flexible to your players' choices. Each piece of advice here - from setting the scene, nudging players with illusionary choices, or balancing risk and reward - is designed to help you create a story that feels alive, responsive, and deeply engaging.

Running a game is as much about adapting as it is about planning. With every session, you're honing a unique skill set that combines storytelling, social awareness, and gameplay mechanics. Whether you're crafting a climactic one-shot or an expansive campaign, you're now better prepared to guide your players through a narrative journey that is both rewarding and fun. Gather your notes, take a deep breath, and step confidently into your next session.

Chapter 4:
Having Fun

If you're not having fun as a DM, then what's the point? Sure, you're juggling storylines, characters, and rules, plus trying to keep your players on track (while they're trying their hardest to derail you). But at the end of the day, DMing is as much about your enjoyment as it is theirs.

Being a DM is like directing a movie where the actors keep rewriting the script. You're not just watching the story unfold—you're steering it, adding surprises, and reacting to all the ridiculous things your players throw at you. It's about leaning into the chaos, having some laughs, and building something memorable together.

It's worth pointing out that having fun as a DM doesn't look the same for everyone. Maybe you're here for the drama and epic speeches, or perhaps you're all about rolling dice and combat strategy. Either way, you get to blend your style with what keeps your players engaged.

Finding Your DM Style

So, you've come this far. You've seen your players grapple with goblins, bicker with barkeeps, and possibly commit a few "unintended" arsons (hopefully in-game), but now it's time to consider what kind of Dungeon Master you are. Finding your DM style isn't about picking a fixed point on a path and standing on it - it's about finding the blend of techniques that allow you and your players to traverse the path together while having the most fun.

There are two general styles DMs tend to gravitate toward: Narrative-Driven and Rules-Oriented. Instead of viewing these styles as two separate paths, try to view them as two intertwined paths that break off into countless smaller trails, splitting apart and rejoining together at random intervals. This path is your campaign.

These paths blend together and lead to the same destination, so although you could strictly follow one or the other, it's often easier and more fulfilling to choose whichever seems to be easier to travel on or seems to be a more direct route forward. Some tables may prefer character development and cool action setpieces, leaning more toward the Narrative-Driven path. While other tables may prefer to make decisions based on how they interpret the written game rules, favoring the Rules-Oriented path.

Before my metaphor falls apart -if it hasn't already- I'd like to explain in more detail the distinctions between the two styles so you are able to more easily choose your personal blend.

The Narrative-Driven DM

Hearing a fragment of a sentence and being able to envision a scene immediately is a hallmark of narrative-driven DMs. Not only are these Dungeon Masters able to imagine what that scene looks like, but they also know *exactly* how to convey it with words. They will likely choose to evoke the senses by describing the smell of roasted chicken and spilled beer along with the visual of the tavern lit by a crackling fireplace and torches scattered along the walls as the bard sings his sad melody and the rowdy crowd jeers him.

You have a lot of opportunities to evoke emotions in your players when using the narrative approach, and that might be the exact experience some of them are looking for. You can also control the pace with these touching character moments or descriptions of quaint locations. Don't overwhelm them with too much detail, lest you find yourself narrating a scene while the Barbarian's player whispers, "When do I get to smash something?"

The important thing to remember is what I said in chapter two about structuring a session. Having an intriguing hook, a surprising twist, and a satisfying conclusion is critical to having an excellent narrative-driven session.

Still, this style also offers you a lot of room to adapt and improvise. In fact, you *should* prepare in advance for possible shifts in the story because a narrative-driven session offers many opportunities for players to explore and branch off in unexpected directions.

This preparation is important because, thanks to the flexibility of this approach, it allows you to create something memorable.

At the same time, it ties back to the idea of rewards I discussed earlier. With a narrative-driven approach, the focus is on character growth and player agency - elements that can be challenging to manage if you're new to DMing. So, if this feels daunting, consider leaning toward a more rules-oriented style, which provides a clearer structure to guide players through the story while you gain confidence in your narrative skills.

The Rules-Oriented DM

On the other side of the scale, we have the Rules-Oriented DM. This is the DM who treats the Player's Handbook like a holy relic and can use their photographic memory to recite exact definitions of spells and items, like a five-year-old who can belt out every lyric of *Let it Go*. If the game goes off track, this DM is ready with precise spell ranges, saving throws, and perhaps even a pre-prepared flowchart. Think of them like a film director framing a perfect shot— everything has to work as it's written, or it's just chaos.

This approach is fantastic for players who want a predictable, fair experience where everyone's on an even playing field. Admittedly, that might make you feel like an overly pedantic referee looking to sanction every little infraction. Trust me, you don't want to be that guy. Admittedly, flexibility isn't the strongest suit when following rules, which is why you should be careful how strictly you follow them when your players are trying something creative.

Being a rules-oriented DM might sound like being a Rules Lawyer with extra steps, but it isn't. It ensures fairness and balance in encounters, so you'll never have to worry about this DM having an agenda against you or other players. In a game like *D&D*, there is a clear system of calculating encounter difficulty, and you can bet your bottom dollar that this DM will have that balance before you enter combat. Or, they might use an especially difficult encounter to move players away from a section of the campaign they're not meant to reach until later.

Of course, using this approach would require extremely strict consistency in your rulings, both for your players and NPCs. And while being a stickler for the rules can be a desirable situation in the right circumstances, it also creates room for exploitation. For example, your players may know a monster's stats and will, therefore, know how to defeat it. This is called metagaming, which means that players use the knowledge they have from outside the game their character wouldn't have inside the game. Many DMs strongly discourage and even outwardly punish metagaming because it hurts the session as a whole for both players and the DM, giving more experienced players an unfair advantage while making the DM's life much harder.

The main drawback of being focused on the rules is reduced flexibility in storytelling, and if you limit player actions that fall within some of the more loosely defined rules, they may feel restricted, discouraging them from being creative.

As you could've gathered, this approach is better for players who enjoy strictly defined rules of combat mechanics and may not enjoy social interactions or exploration. Still, most players will enjoy aspects of both approaches, which is why it's essential to understand how you can mix and match what you need.

Blending Both Styles

Most DMs aren't purely narrative-driven or strictly rules-oriented. You're not required to pick a side and stick to it, like some rigid alignment in a character sheet. Instead, think of your style as a fluid mix, shifting depending on the session, the group, or even just your mood. Some sessions may call for immersive, story-rich elements to build tension and draw your players into the plot, and other times, a straightforward, mechanics-focused approach is exactly what the party needs to enjoy the game.

Being a balanced DM means knowing when to combine the two styles or shift one into the other. It's like being a jack of all trades, which means you're adaptable enough to deliver a memorable experience, whether it's epic storytelling or strategic combat. Mastering this balance is what keeps your game versatile and responsive, allowing you to lean towards one style or another based on what will enhance the moment. This will let your players feel like every session fits exactly what they're in the mood for.

Remember that no one style is better than the other - it's about what serves the game and your style best at any given moment. The most memorable sessions often come from a seamless blend of the two approaches, where you weave story elements into combat or use rules to guide players' interactions with the narrative. Letting yourself experiment with both styles - and learning when to use each one - gives you the flexibility to adapt to any scenario your players throw your way.

Ultimately, developing this balance should create a game experience that keeps everyone at the table engaged, yourself included, and the best way to achieve it is to have an open and honest discussion with your players.

Accepting Feedback

As a DM, you *want* to hear what your players have to say about your session, even when they aren't giving you the praise you believe you deserve. If your players aren't giving you enough feedback, be sure to ask them for it yourself. But honestly, you shouldn't *have* to ask; you're far more likely to get sick of your players' opinions than need to ask for more.

There is a right and wrong way to give feedback, but this doesn't mean that your players will always give it in the 'correct' way. As a DM, it's your job not only to learn to take critiques in a positive light without getting your ego bruised but also to (at least try to) teach your players constructive ways to give criticism.

Sometimes, players - for various reasons - will choose to withhold feedback about your session, especially if the feedback is negative. They may be worried about confrontation, or they may just be sensitive to your emotions and be worried about hurting your feelings. If your players don't voluntarily give you their opinion on your session, ask them directly and assure them you can handle whatever they have to throw at you- just make sure you pick the right time.

When's the Right Time for Q&A

So far, I have only discussed talking about the game with your players during Session Zero, but when it comes to feedback, it's best to have a talk with your players *after* you finish playing, just not *immediately after* the session is over.

The main reason why you would want to talk to your players after some time has passed (be it a few hours, days, or even weeks) instead of immediately after is to allow your session to settle. Without an adequate amount of time to reflect upon the session, your player's opinions could still be directly influenced by the game they just played. This immediate return information might even send you in a completely wrong direction when planning your next session.

Now, the issue with waiting to get feedback is that you'll have to track down your players individually to get it, which is time-consuming and annoying. If this feels a little bit like a catch-22, it's because it is. There simply isn't a perfect way to get the right feedback, which is why I try to get feedback immediately after the session and then follow up later in the week if I feel my players have been shell-shocked from the barrage of twists and turns I aimed their way during our session.

You *can* go without feedback, but I wouldn't recommend it. After all, knowing how your players react to your DMing style and adjust is the best way to grow and improve as a Dungeon Master.

Feedback as a Tool for Growth

Constructive feedback is awesome - if given kindly and taken humbly. As a DM, you're often deeply invested in your sessions, crafting fulfilling stories, exciting encounters, and unexpected twists. Still, sometimes, your players may have different ideas about what makes the game engaging. Perhaps they want more action, more social interaction, or just a chance to have a say in the story's direction. Listening to their thoughts and making adjustments can keep everyone at the table engaged without sacrificing the vision you bring as a DM.

When players share feedback, focus on what's in your control *and* practical. For example, if they mention that combat feels a bit slow, consider ways to streamline turns or adjust encounter difficulty to keep the energy up. Or, if they express a desire for more NPC interactions, think about adding a few recurring characters with whom they can interact and develop bonds. Minor tweaks can make your game more immersive and keep players excited to return each week.

It's also helpful to remember that feedback isn't a critique of *you*; it's insight into what's working and what you could improve. Players often quickly share what they love - be it a tense cliffhanger, a thought-provoking puzzle, or a well-designed encounter - and by paying attention to what draws their attention, you'll learn what resonates most with them. Then, when they give you constructive pointers on pacing or encounters, you'll have a sense of what keeps them engaged and can adapt accordingly.

The best campaigns are built on collaboration. By showing your players their feedback is valued, you create a sense of shared investment in the story you're building together. Not only will they feel more involved, but you'll grow as a DM, discovering new ways to enhance your sessions and meet your players where they are. Accepting and integrating feedback gracefully is a skill that makes you not just a better DM but a better storyteller and game leader overall.

How to Handle Tough Criticism

Not all feedback is sunshine and rainbows. Inevitably, a player will bring up something they didn't enjoy - and when that happens, it can sting. After all, you've put hours of thought, planning, and energy into crafting something special, and it's natural to feel a bit deflated if players don't see it the way you do. Feedback, even the tough kind, is part of the process because it's there to help you grow as a DM and make your game better.

The goal is to take what's valid from the critique without letting it rattle your confidence because not every comment will be equally constructive, and not every suggestion will align with your vision.

So, if a player mentions that they're not a fan of how you handled something, try to see it as an opportunity to improve as a DM rather than a critique of your abilities. The key is to find what is helpful in their feedback, even when harsh or unconstructive, turning it into something you can build on.

Sometimes, though, feedback will feel especially harsh and borderline personal. Maybe a player didn't love a major plot twist you introduced, or perhaps they found an encounter frustrating rather than challenging. In those moments, remind yourself that you're running a game, not crafting a perfect, mistake-free experience. Games are unpredictable by nature, and well, *stuff* happens. It's okay if every session isn't flawless - after all, some of the best stories come from unexpected twists and even outright failures.

Let me be real here for a moment - *every* DM has moments where they roll a "natural one," whether with storytelling, pacing, or overall decision-making. When criticism feels like a personal attack, just remember that, most often, it isn't. The player is most likely frustrated and is venting and just isn't being pleasant.

However, if you come into the game mentally prepared for something like that, you'll be far more likely to find a way to turn that into something constructive.

The game is as much a learning experience for you as it is for your players, and each session gives you a new chance to experiment with new techniques, adjust genres, and improve your improvisation skills. When you view feedback as part of this process rather than a judgment, it becomes a powerful tool to refine your approach.

At the end of the day, feedback - especially the critical kind - is how you make lemons into lemonade. Players may have valid points that can elevate your DM game, and it's up to you to do the heavy lifting and use these points to elevate it.

If you're struggling to cope with critical feedback, consider encouraging your players to use the 'feedback sandwich' method, a common strategy used to give notes to scriptwriters (who are often very emotionally invested in the stories they have written), which involves layering critical statements (the sandwich meat) between two positive statements (the bread) for an easier-to-swallow, constructive approach that won't shatter anyone's dreams.

Using a 'feedback sandwich' may seem a bit excessive to those familiar with the concept. While, yes, it may be overdoing it a little, it's useful because, as a rookie DM (and an 'average' human), you're likely to be anxious about receiving feedback and getting your players to phrase it as a 'sandwich' is a great way to absorb all the necessary information without making you feel like a total failure and a disappointment to the spirit of the late Gary Gygax.

I understand this exact approach is unrealistic for 90 percent of groups - I know none of my parties do it (despite my constant pleading). The important thing is that you *Inception* your players into layering different types of feedback so you can more easily digest it. Sure, they might work together to deliver you a triple-quadruple-decker-ultimate-supreme-meatlover's-heartattack-express-sandwich with extra cheese... and a *diet* coke, but even if that's the case, at least you made them *try* to remain conscious of how they structure their feedback, which was your true goal all along.

Learning how to embrace feedback, both positive and critical, is a mark of a great DM. Showing your players that their opinions matter will build trust and respect, causing them to be more invested in the game.

It'll also give them an opportunity to return that trust when you try something new. Accepting feedback gracefully isn't just about improving your sessions; it's about cultivating a collaborative atmosphere that makes everyone feel heard. Over time, you'll develop the skill to take feedback in stride, turn it into actionable changes, and maybe even look forward to those "constructive" conversations. Then, it may be time to...

Challenge Yourself

Once you've found your groove as a DM, things can start to feel predictable. Your players might form stereotypes because they'll know what to expect: the Rogue will try to steal from every merchant, the Barbarian will smash, and the Bard... Well... he'll also smash. When you reach this stage, it's time to spice things up and push yourself beyond your comfort zone.

Maybe this is when you want to let *that* player create his chaotic evil character. Who knows, maybe you want to have a whole party full of evil characters who, instead of looking to have a heroic story, will want to run your fictional world as ultimate villains.

Or perhaps it is *you* who found the high fantasy a tad *too* high and want to switch to something more realistic. Just don't overshoot it and send your wizards and paladins to the crime-ridden Chicago during the prohibition era. Or maybe do *exactly* that. I'm sure Al Capone would have *loved* to have had a wizard in his ranks. Not sure how the paladin would feel about it, though.

Hey, who knows - maybe now's the time to try that 1920s gangster accent you always wanted to do. But skip the Italian hand gestures. Capiche?

Trying New Genres

One great way to challenge yourself as a DM is to try out a new genre. If you're used to running classic high fantasy campaigns with elves, dragons, and enchanted forests, consider a one-shot in a gritty noir setting or a sci-fi space opera. Suddenly, your familiar tropes get a facelift - the grizzled tavern keeper becomes a shady informant in a trench coat, and the Barbarian transforms into a cyborg who has catchphrases of "Get to the choppa" and "I'll be back.". This shift in setting can completely change the feel of your game, offering you and your players a refreshing new experience.

Switching genres keeps things fresh for everyone at the table. Players who may have fallen into a routine with their characters will find themselves approaching challenges differently, adapting to unfamiliar settings and new social norms. For you, each genre comes with its own set of storytelling and improvisational challenges. A sci-fi setting, for instance, might lean into futuristic tech and alien diplomacy, while a noir-inspired game could involve mysterious crimes, shadowy figures, and intricate webs of betrayal. Experimenting with different genres helps you develop versatility as a DM, keeping everybody at the table engaged.

Genre-swapping is also an effective way to expand your DM skills. Each genre has its own "feel," and by trying new settings, you can broaden your repertoire and find ways to deliver unique tones and atmospheres. Running a horror session, for example, may focus on building suspense and eerie encounters, whereas a comedy-themed game relies more on quick-thinking improvisation and absurd scenarios. Learning how to adapt your storytelling style to these different tones can boost your confidence and enhance your ability to create engaging experiences, no matter the setting.

Switching genres mid-campaign can add variety, but doing so without warning can feel abrupt or confusing. While players may sometimes appreciate the change, it's best to approach it thoughtfully and communicate openly. A good time to discuss a genre shift is during natural story pauses - after a major arc wraps up or when introducing a new plot thread. This way, the transition feels purposeful rather than disruptive.

Regular check-ins with players outside of gameplay are invaluable to keep everyone on the same page. You might ask them how they're feeling about the current tone, whether they'd be interested in exploring a different vibe, or if there's anything they'd like to see more of. This kind of feedback loop not only ensures your genre shifts (or any major changes) align with their interests but also helps build trust, making players more invested and engaged in the evolving story.

However, there are situations where changing the genre can work well. One such example is if you wanted to switch the genre by using it as a twist in the story.

Maybe your players went looking for a magical item that transported them from their classic medieval-inspired swords-and-sorcery setting to 1920s Manhattan, where Eldritch horrors are relentlessly hunting them down.

Twisting the story can have other functions, as well. Personally, I might even overuse this, but I like changing things up with new story twists - whether it's a genre switch or a new gameplay twist.

Experimenting with New Techniques

Part of challenging yourself as a DM is pushing the boundaries on gameplay techniques. Maybe you try running a session with no dice at all - where every outcome is based purely on roleplay and player decisions. Or you can build a true open-world sandbox where the players can go anywhere and do anything, leaving the familiar structured adventure format behind. These new approaches can feel like running through a dark forest, but that's what makes them exciting. They can open up entirely new ways to tell the story and keep everyone at the table on their toes.

Exploring new ways to run a tabletop RPG session often means branching out into entirely new systems—

a point we touched on back in Chapter One. If you find yourself gravitating towards specific mechanics or themes, consider diving into a game system tailored to bring those elements to life. After all, this guide isn't just about D&D—it's about discovering the potential of all TTRPGs, and a new system may be the perfect path to achieve the exact effect of excitement and change you've been looking for without the need to majorly adjust game mechanics.

The more techniques you try, the more adaptable you become. A session without dice can draw players deep into a story where everything flows from their choices instead of the luck of the roll. It's a great way to encourage roleplay and character interaction, especially when everyone's in the mood to dig into the narrative. A sandbox, on the other hand, throws *you* in with them, reacting on the fly as they make choices you didn't see coming. It can feel intense, but this style builds your improvisation skills and forces you to be quick on your feet, ready for any twist they throw your way.

Trying out new techniques also brings out different sides of your players. A session all about roleplay might pull quieter players into the spotlight, giving them space to explore their character more. A sandbox setup lets the adventurous players cut loose, seeing where they can go when allowed to roam free. If you remain flexible in your approach, you can let your battle berserkers thrive in combat, silver-tongued rogues slither their way through role-playing, and adventurers explore far corners of your world - while witnessing unparalleled immersion at the same time.

Plus, mixing up techniques keeps things from feeling too sterilized - you want your players to come to each session knowing they can expect the unexpected. Maybe you run a session entirely in character, with players relying solely on what their characters know, or you try a world-building night where the players add to the setting themselves. These kinds of experiments don't just expand your skills - they also keep your players engaged and hungry for more, knowing every session might hold a surprise.

Experimenting with techniques is about gradually expanding your comfort zone and bringing variety to the game because you're not just telling a story; you're creating an experience that feels different each time you sit down together. So don't be afraid to throw out the usual playbook every now and then. Every time you try something new, you're giving your players a fresh adventure - and making yourself an even better DM.

Growing Your Improvisation Skills

The skill of improvisation is a cornerstone for any DM, which improves significantly with experience. Initially, you may rely on detailed notes, scripted dialogue, and pre-planned encounters to feel prepared. Over time, however, you'll grow more comfortable trusting your instincts and might even relish the unpredictability of going off-script. And let's be honest, players will give you plenty of chances. They'll inevitably ask about the history of a random street vendor's wares or decide that the ogre guarding the treasure might actually be friendship material. Being able to roll with it and adapt to their whims keeps the game vibrant and responsive - and it's a skill that will transform your sessions.

As your improvisation improves, you'll notice how much it enriches your world. Let's say your players stumble upon a cursed object, and they start asking questions that your notes don't cover. Instead of scrambling, tap into your imagination and conjure up a mysterious backstory on the spot. This spontaneous lore adds depth to the world you're creating, and you can weave it back into the plot later if it sparks their interest. Improvising in these moments not only keeps players engaged but also allows you to build out your setting in surprising and organic ways.

The more you embrace improvisation, the more confident you'll feel to allow your players' choices to shape the story. When they throw curveballs, like pursuing an unexpected NPC alliance or following a weird side quest, your ability to adapt allows those choices to become part of the fabric of the story. Players love the feeling that their choices truly matter, and responding to their ideas in real time will strengthen their investment in the story. It's a skill that builds trust because your players will come to see the world as an open playground where their actions have an actual impact.

So, as you keep DMing, try to lean into those moments when things go off-script. Improvisation isn't about discarding your prep; it's about blending it with in-the-moment creativity to create a session that's as dynamic as your players' imaginations. The more you practice, the easier it gets to take a deep breath, trust your instincts, and let the story unfold in ways you never anticipated. And before you know it, those improvised details will start to feel like essential parts of your game world.

Creating a Long Campaign

So, you've mastered the art of the one-shot; short adventures are second nature by now, and you feel ready to move on to a more prolonged sprawling story. This is where you move beyond isolated stories and begin crafting a more extensive, cohesive world that your players can explore and shape. In a long campaign, characters aren't just passing through; they're growing, building connections, and leaving lasting impacts. Here, the magic lies not only in the narrative twists or thrilling encounters but in the unfolding history your group creates together, one session at a time.

In the following sections, I'll be giving you some *baseline* advice on how to craft a longer campaign, but our team has *far* more advice up our sleeves. If you decide you like what you're about to read, be sure to check out our next book, *The Advanced RPG Guide to Becoming an Expert Dungeon Master*.

The entire book is structured around building and running long-term campaigns. It begins with a crash course into worldbuilding and homebrewing (which we will *also* be developing further in future books) and then transitions into the art of designing a campaign for longevity, keeping the momentum going over the sessions, as well as managing the ever-evolving complexity of the world, players' choices, and campaign as a whole. We'll even teach you how to transport your players directly into your campaign through apt background music and special effects, such as mood lighting, that craft the perfect atmosphere.

Trust me, if you're looking to level up your DMing abilities and become a master storyteller while simultaneously developing your own unique style, *The Advanced RPG Guide to Becoming an Expert Dungeon Master* is a must-read for you!

Start with the End in Mind

Planning a long campaign means laying down a vision. Think of it as a rough map of where things might end up, even if the route itself changes along the way. You might envision the players eventually saving a kingdom from a rising evil, uncovering a conspiracy that only they can expose, or confronting a nemesis that has haunted them from the beginning. Knowing the destination doesn't mean controlling every step; it's about guiding players toward their goal over the horizon. Having a loose ending in mind keeps the story cohesive and ensures that even the wildest of detours will find their way back to a satisfying conclusion. So keep things flexible and let your players' choices influence how you get to that final point because it is the journey that truly gives the ending its weight.

Believe it or not, starting with an end in mind isn't all that different from a one-shot, but in this and the following few sections, we'll dive into the art of crafting longer campaigns - sprawling stories that unfold over time, leaving a lasting impact.

The beauty of a long campaign is that it doesn't require a rigid plot. You don't have to steer players down a single path to reach your planned finale. Instead, create opportunities for their choices to matter, crafting a story that responds to their actions. Subtly foreshadow the ending by planting hints or encounters that will gain meaning later. Some players might catch on, while others may not, but when everything comes together, the payoff feels earned. By allowing player choices to shape their path, you create a shared story that feels both personal and epic.

Keeping the Momentum

One of the greatest challenges of long campaigns is keeping everyone engaged. A slow or repetitive arc can make a campaign feel stagnant, and without smaller and easier goals for players to accomplish, even the most committed ones can lose steam. Think of each session like an episode in a TV show - it doesn't need to advance the main plot, but it should still feel satisfying on its own. Small wins, individual side-quests, and mini-arcs can help keep the momentum alive. These shorter stories within the campaign allow players to feel a sense of progress even when the main plot unfolds more slowly.

Variety is vital to keeping things fresh. You can change up the tone with occasional surprises: perhaps a trusted ally turns traitor, a new villain appears, or the party encounters a mysterious faction. Twists and new elements not only add depth but also keep the players on their toes, so make use of world events, player backstories, or new NPCs to create new directions for the party. Keeping players guessing and giving them new things to uncover will keep them eager to return week after week, investing more of themselves in the story as it unfolds.

Adapting to Character Development

One of the joys of long campaigns is watching the characters evolve. These aren't static heroes who reset each week - they're adventurers whose pasts, personalities, and values evolve as they face new challenges. As a DM, your role isn't just to set the scene but to respond to the ways characters change. Maybe the Barbarian starts off as a blunt instrument of destruction but slowly develops a softer side, building connections with villagers or forging bonds with other party members. Perhaps the Rogue, initially driven by greed, finds a cause worth fighting for, shifting from a lone wolf to a team player. Maybe even the Bard changes, going from his previous form of smashing, to the type that uses a mace.

Recognizing and supporting these changes enriches the story. Character growth can become as significant as the main plot itself, with players discovering new layers of their heroes. Who knows, they may discover they're more similar to ogres than they thought.

If a character's arc starts pulling them in a new direction, adapt the story to incorporate that shift. Maybe a personal conflict leads to a side quest, or a moral dilemma creates tension within the party. The campaign becomes not only about the world-saving quest but also about each character's journey as their lives intertwine. Encouraging and weaving character development into the main story lets players experience the full weight of their decisions, making the world feel alive and responsive.

Building Toward Major Twists and a Satisfying Conclusion

A long campaign is ripe with opportunities for big reveals and memorable twists. When players invest time and energy into a story, they'll remember the moments that surprised them, the revelations that changed their perspective, and the climactic battles that felt truly epic. Plan a few major twists that build on elements of the story they thought they understood - an NPC who isn't who they seemed, a magical artifact with unforeseen consequences, or a long-hidden secret that redefines the quest.

As the campaign nears its end, it's time to tie these elements together, creating a satisfying finale. Call back to earlier sessions, bringing back familiar faces, references, and story arcs that made the journey meaningful. The finale is your chance to reflect on the players' entire journey, honoring their choices and showing how they've shaped the world.

When done well, it's a send-off they'll remember - a culmination of their shared experiences, complete with high stakes, familiar faces, and, if you're lucky, a few tears. When done poorly, you'll be happy if they forget it in a week and don't bring up the time you tried to end a two-year-long campaign with "the butler did it" just to witness you cringing in shame. Stop judging me! It's a perfectly reasonable situation that could've happened to anyone.

Creating a long campaign is no small feat, whether from scratch or building off of somebody else's, but it's one of the most rewarding experiences for a DM - especially because, by now, you've had to improvise enough that you've truly made this campaign your own. As your players grow into their characters, build friendships (or rivalries), and face their fears, you'll watch them build a story that's uniquely theirs. And as you learn to adapt, evolve, and bring the world to life, you'll see your own growth as well. So take a deep breath, set your sights on that ending, and get ready for an adventure as epic as the journey you're creating for your players. Speaking of endings...

Recap

If you learned anything from this chapter (and this whole book for that matter), it is that DMing should be fun, both for you and your players... Oh! And you had better start by running that one-shot or... dishonor on your whole family! Dishonor on you! Dishonor on your cow! Just start with the one-shot! Imagine DMing not just as a responsibility to juggle rules, characters, and storylines but as a shared adventure where everyone at the table has a great time. Lean into the unpredictable chaos that players bring, laugh at the unexpected, and remember - DMing is about creating something unforgettable together.

Finding your DM style can take time, but it is the logical next step. Are you more like a movie director, crafting a story with rich, immersive scenes, memorable side characters with great one-liners, and action-packed endings, or are you closer to a game designer dedicated to robust and effective level design, upholding rules and balance, while providing satisfying gameplay? Your DM style might lean more one way than the other, but it doesn't have to be fixed. Instead, think of it as a blend, a spectrum that you can adjust with each campaign based on the preferences of your players and the type of tale you want to tell. Embracing this flexibility can elevate your game, giving each session a distinct flavor that keeps everyone engaged. Not only that, but it can help you improve your DMing skills - and trust me, no matter how many times you run a session, you can *always* improve.

Learning to blend these styles is a valuable skill. Some sessions may call for dramatic storytelling, while others will benefit from straightforward mechanics. A good DM doesn't cling rigidly to one style but knows when to shift gears, adapting to the flow of the game and the mood of the players, and it is precisely this versatility that can help you tailor each session to be as memorable as possible.

Receiving feedback from your players is part of this journey, and while not all feedback may be glowing, it's an essential tool for growth. Players often know what resonates with them, whether it's more action, deeper roleplay, or faster combat. Taking their constructive feedback lets you refine your approach, shaping a game that stays engaging without losing your personal style. Going a step further and embracing feedback, both positive and critical, builds a collaborative atmosphere where players feel heard and invested in the game, enhancing the experience for everyone.

Once you find your groove, challenge yourself by trying out new genres, experimenting with fresh techniques, and embracing improvisation. This keeps the game dynamic and prevents it from becoming stale. Such experiments aren't just for variety - they're tools to improve your DM skills, enhancing your ability to create a game world that feels alive and responsive to your players' choices.

The chapter also peaked into the intricacies of running a long campaign. With a sprawling storyline, you'll craft a cohesive world where characters grow, relationships deepen, and choices leave lasting impacts. Starting with a loose ending in mind gives direction, but it's the journey - as always - that makes it meaningful. Keeping the momentum alive, especially in a long campaign, involves balancing the main plot with smaller goals and surprising twists to keep players invested week after week.

Long campaigns can also be about character development, where each character's growth adds weight to the story. Adapting to these changes can keep the game dynamic and ensure that players feel their choices have real consequences. As the campaign builds toward its conclusion, weaving in callbacks, twists, and story arcs makes the finale feel earned, a culmination of every experience shared along the way.

Now that my team and I have taught you everything you need to know to begin running tabletop role-playing games in your role as the Dungeon Master - be sure to have fun and not stress! Mistakes will happen, but that is okay! What RPGs are really all about is crafting a shared story with your friends —an epic journey shaped by the entire table, one memorable session at a time.

But before you start playing, we need to ask you one more thing: please leave an Amazon review for our book. It may seem a bit selfish of us to ask, but if we don't please our algorithmic overlords our adventure will be over before it's started. All we ask is for a minute of your time to help us out for free; you've already spent hours of your time reading this book, and if you've made it this far, you must've enjoyed it, so what's one minute more? To leave us a review, just scan the code on the next page and click on *The Advanced RPG Beginners Guide to Becoming a Dungeon Master*.

Thank you for taking the time to read our guide. We hope to see you again in our next book, where we teach you to level up your Dungeon Master skills from beginner to expert. And always be sure to remember... start with that one-shot! :)

Made in the USA
Middletown, DE
10 February 2025

71065381R00103